# APASTORAL

a mistopia

# A NOVEL

Lee D. Thompson

corona/samizdat 2022

*Apastoral: A Mistopia*

Copyright © 2022 by Lee D. Thompson
Introduction by Jeff Bursey, Copyright © 2022

Cover Art and Typesetting by Galleon Publishing
Illustrations, Adobe Stock

Published by corona\samizdat, Izola, Slovenia
Chief Editor: Rick Harsch

Printed by request in the EU, 2022, by Primitus d.o.o.

*CIP - Kataložni zapis o publikaciji*
*Narodna in univerzitetna knjižnica, Ljubljana*
*821.111-31*
*THOMPSON, Lee D., 1968-*
  *Apastoral : a mistopia / Lee D. Thompson ; [illustrations Adobe Stock].*
*- Izola : Corona samizdat, 2022*
*ISBN 978-961-95863-0-3*
*COBISS.SI-ID 113991171*

*All rights reserved. No part of this publication can be used in any way without prior written permission of the publisher, except for quotes, reviews, and other non-commercial uses permitted by copyright law.*

# Woolgathering in the Atlantic Provinces; or, The Introduction to Lee D. Thompson's *Apastoral: A Mistopia*

By Jeff Bursey

Lee Thompson and I go back some years, and so these pages before the main event are going to be personal and pointed.

It's often true that writers who become friends and get together now and then, as when I lived in Prince Edward Island and Lee lived, as he has for most of his life, in New Brunswick, if they share enthusiasms, for Joseph McElroy, for guitars, for the offbeat, and are surrounded by those, writers or not, who don't have the same interests, likely will ask more of each other as time goes on. Like Lee asking me at a last minute for this introduction, and on a holiday no less. So that's why there's the definite article and not some coy "an."

Turned out that Lee and I demand more from books, especially by people we know, than most others in our circles, and to my mind that's fine, though it can be interpreted as wanting something more, or other, from a person, not just the author. It can get tricky when we like, or just know, the people we read; if what we say about their work upsets them, then there you are, and either that lasts or else there's forgiveness. A big fruit basket can do wonders.

When I read *Apastoral* in manuscript I knew from the opening that here was something that appealed, like the work of Chris Eaton, to my sensibilities. It's not at all like Wallace and Gromit, though it does have its share of incompetents and characters who are clowns when not cons. In the context of Canadian literature (or CanLit, as it's called in this country) its humour is sickening, in the best ways, and dark. It has funny lines, as much of Lee's work does. The acidic nature of this novel, its scepticism and anger, its view of society, government, relationships, science, nature, and individual identity as states of being with no permanence, mean that few of the characters are loveable. What does loveable mean? Fuzzy feelings, the kind that encourage sales and garner attention for prizes. The kind of writing that provokes kisses from marketing departments and publicists and tears in the eyes from sappy booksellers and librarians. The small presses in Canada are indistinguishable from the big presses when it comes to these things. They're all pot and no lobster, to use a good old Atlantic Canadian expression. Or, in this book's agro-parlance, they're mutton dressed up as lamb. I know I don't create characters you feel like pecking on the back of the neck—indeed, my books have caused people, people Lee knows, not to speak to me after they've been read or after I've given a reading—so Lee and I share this marketing fault.

We bonded over writers, and then strengthened those ties by reading the other's works from time to time and getting to see that the proof of our professed convictions, what made us unmarketable, what made Book*hug (you likely think this can't possibly be the name of a real publishing house) or Invisible reject us, sprang from the lines, from the inventiveness, of writers content (we fucking had to be, I suppose) to go our own way, for however long it took until someone noticed.

And now, here Lee is. But he's been noticed for years by anyone who's read his novel (or is it a biography?) *S., a novel in [xxx] dreams*, who's come across his stories as they appear in journals, who's heard his self-penned tunes, seen their own stories come out under his editing hand in his on-and-off-again journal *Galleon*, or been the grateful recipient of an invitation to read at this or that venue in Moncton alongside other writers. He built community in a place that welcomes that kind of effort.

*Apastoral* has community, too. Unfortunately for the characters, but thankfully for us, it's a picture of a penal colony and attitudes behind incarceration found in Canada and the U.S. What it says about society is not quite sidelong, but it is absurd and disgusted. By the end what we have left are the bones, if you will, of people, not fully fleshed humans, or even sheep. This deliberate approach can be off-putting. Yet there are so many readers who want something different not for novelty's sake but to learn about or hear of a new way to look at things. This is a novel that's bleak and funny, downbeat but bumptious. You can see Lee inverting mores, ideas, professions, moods, logic, and the bestial nature of the human animal in ways that says *this is all madness!* in language that has verve and in images that remain in the mind long after the last page is read.

While reading Gabriel Josipovici's novel *Infinity* I came across these lines: "Sheep without the innocence of sheep. Sheep without the kindly disposition of sheep." How true to *Apastoral* these words are. It's a book I wish I could read for the first time once again. But a second reading has its own pungent pleasures.

Edmonton, July 1, 2022

# Part One

## Hanged for a Sheep as for a Lamb

*Unnatural Things*

No one knows what triggers it, that waking connection between hindbrain and forebrain, that spark firing across a foggy gap. One moment you're a happy pony with simple desires—run, leap, chase—and next moment you're reliving the axe swinging through a soft skull. One moment you're a glutinous pig chasing sumptuous sows—and the next moment you're planning their vivisection. And one moment you're a sleepy sheep chewing weeds in a field of flowers, savouring the green-green, mildly annoyed by the fly biting your ass, and the next you're possessed by a lingering sense of injustice. The flowers lose their colour, and the fly is every tormentor you've ever known.

For me, sleepy sheep, the mist lifted one morning when I heard the cock crow and found myself wondering why the dumb bird would want to wake those murderers. I knew the door would swing open and the chickens gathered for slaughter and that stupid fucking rooster would do it again and again, morning after morning, rain or shine. One had to have a word with the piss-brained thing, or give it a good stomping. So I trotted over to where it was perched on the red tractor, shitting mindlessly on the dew-wet seat, and things started to come together. I don't know why they started to come together then, but the rooster looked at me, cocked its hideous head, skittered a bit, stopped, and waited. And I opened my mouth, wanting to tell it to go stick its shrivelled head into the dim pink of a cow's rectum, but I couldn't. What came out was monosyllabic and not human. I tried again, but the same sound came, maybe a little higher pitched this time, and although the noise made the rooster jump and scamper, that wasn't my intention.

Come back, shit for brains. Explain yourself! Have you no conscience? Just gets up there and squawks *good morning! come murder my girls! come chop their heads off! good morning! good morning!* So I chased him behind the barn but he slipped under the fence and out into the field, feathers flying and a riot of clucking.

And there I was, standing before two thin lines of barbwire fence, wooden fence posts nearly falling over. Part of my mind was telling me this was an insurmountable barrier, and another said that I was in error. Error. That was such an odd word to appear. And then the word terror appeared and I tell you, if I hadn't been standing on my own four feet I would have toppled over, would have lain belly up staring at the sun suddenly knowing what that miserable rooster never knew, that the sun was a ball of fire adrift in a vast void, that the earth was a planet orbiting that same ball of fire. I knew it, and I felt more dizzy.

And I knew that some things are unnatural, and I was one of those unnatural things.

## *A Brief History of Constock*

Let's talk about Constock. Let's get a grasp on who I am, what I am. Oh, it's a wonderful source of jokes, isn't it? Who hasn't made a Constock joke, one that always ends in someone's great embarrassment or shame? A Constock on parole walks into a bar and orders a drink, asks for a—dot dot dot—*scotch*. Bartender says, What's with the pause? Get it? Paws!

Heard about the Constock who crashed the party and no one talked about it? He was the elephant in the room! Constock, if you've been living a hole these past five years, it's what happens when a fed up, right-wing ex-comedian politician takes office and never leaves. It's what happens when crime on the news is rampant and criminals have no fear of punishment, when prisons are the best places to network.

Keep the creeps off our streets, put them in farms!

Lock them up in the craniums of the docile, the meek, put them in pens, *real* pens! Brilliant. Hey, hear about the ex-novelist-turned-Constock? No? Of course not, he wrote under a pen name…

Poor Sylvester Moll. Those dark circles under his eyes, the shaved head of scars. Poor Sylvester would they put him in a cat? No no, his brain wasn't big enough for that. L'il Sillywilly Psychopath they'd put him in a guinea pig, that'd been most fitting.

And the documentary chronicling it all.

Murdered lots of boys, big and small, played no favourites. I do like to kill, he says to the camera, shrugging, only empty in his eyes. Hundred years from now, eh, who remembers? Voice like gravel. Talks of his mother, smiling but sad. Then the image of a quiet farm, then a bright laboratory—this here pig has a tumour, right in the pig brain, and it's all hush hush after that. Commercials. It's unethical, someone shouts after the break, green girl with lice-littered dreadlocks. But look at her reaction when they show pictures of the butchered boys… Still, she says… still… you can't….

Poor Sylvester Moll. I was at Froggies Pub when I first heard what they'd done to him, because for a month we'd heard nothing. Watching the flatscreen, sound drowned in chatter but the pictures telling the story. Sylvester in shackles, the tiny bodies in the ground, the toys, the mittens, the sentencing, the biting of the bailiff's face, the out-of-body glare, the surgeons hunched over a man's head, other surgeons hunched over a pig's head… and lastly a pig with a horrible scar encircling its porcine noggin, blank-eyed pig on a muddy farm happily eating slops.

"Did they really do that?" I said to Weasel. "Did they really do that?"

"You've seen it! It's right there on righteous TV. Is there greater holy fucking proof than that, Bones?"

"They put Moll's brain into…? A pig? They really did it?"

"Crime and punishment! But don't watch that

garbage, man," Weasel said. "Read the newspaper, Bones. Can you even read. These squiggly things?"

And Hog: "Moll? A pig's life? Got off easy."

"But how can they even do that? Wouldn't a man go insane?"

"*That* man?" said Weasel. "Would he know the difference? Anyway, if you're so bloody fascinated with it—"

Arrange a visit, is what he said. Get with the program. Certain memories aren't likely to leave you, and that conversation with Weasel, and that look on his face—mouth open, teeth yellow, annoyed curl in his lips—they're etched deep in my wandering brain. Such things make you wonder about fate, a grand plan with ruts and all, but I don't think fate is the word. It's more like the feeling you're being watched and whatever is watching is a little malicious and entirely churlish. And for the next month, I swear, the entire gang—Hog, Goose, Weasel—would not let it go, and any time I'd show worry or concern about our plan they'd say look, he's worried he'll be baby seal now, whack whack, he's worried they'll squeeze him into duck, quack quack and ha ha, and so on.

Meanwhile, it happened we were at the pub making plans for a little thievery that would set us up for the year, maybe two if we were lucky, because we'd always been lucky. We all agreed we shouldn't go big, that we'd attract too much attention, not so much worried about police but other, nastier elements of criminal society. "We can't step on any toes, right?" says Hog. "Just a small little thing that'll leave us a little richer and a little happier and a little wiser, right? If we believe in it, it'll happen, right?"

Someone must've doubted. Surely it was me.

## *A Giant Leap for Ramkind*

Unnatural me. A barbwire fence. So I used my head, which sadly lacked horns, and pushed the fencepost forward. The base cracked and though the wire tried to hold the post high, it wasn't high, and all I had to do was leap. In the five thousand years of farm animal history had any dumb beast done that? Had any beast thought hard enough to solve the problem? Maybe. Maybe cows do it all the time, when the farmers are sleeping, maybe they hold the wire high while others slip under, carouse all night, return by morning.

No, cows know how to stay out of trouble. Cows don't pace the pasture wondering what the hell went wrong with their lives. Cows don't pause at puddles and consider their reflection. Why do I have these sad eyes? Why do I have these hooves, this heavy body? Why do all my friends disappear without a trace? Have they fled? Where to? And is it better there?

Once on the other side everything came gushing back. And I remembered, yes, yes, that they told me that this would happen. Your old brain will want to become new again, they said, and it will begin to exert control over the sheep's hindbrain, but this could take months. Because firstly, Bones, the body needs to do the body's work, to stay alive, to move about, to breathe, to eat, to defecate and sleep. Yes, it will happen, though it doesn't always happen, the science isn't *perfectly* reliable, but we *want* it to happen, because where is the punishment if you can't remember?

First, you have to remember.

I had died. No: I had been killed. *Murdered.*

But I'm alive.

I looked back to the farm. Through the morning mist two ewes watched me. The prettier of the two, the one with the soulful eyes and the heart-shaped white patch on her forehead, I knew she was considering following me, as much as she could consider anything. I have inside information on this, and consideration, for a sheep, is more like a dance than hopscotch.

I wanted to make a lasting final impression, but I worried I would lose control of my unnatural nature, that I'd start to walk on my hind legs, seek out clothing and lose the desire to nibble on weeds, and that I'd think too much about it: are they poison, will I go into convulsions, die, and be slaughtered? Will I starve? And I had enough sense to begin to worry about wolves and coyotes, yet I had enough sense to know that this was farmland, not the wild, and I'd more likely be shot by drunk college kids, assaulted by lonely farmers, or run over by a tourism bus. I wanted to return to the flock but then I looked at the flock and I no longer wanted to return to the flock.

I bleated farewell to the ewe with soulful eyes.

Surely I sounded like an impostor.

## *Cold as Heist*

I never wanted a life of crime, but I don't recall anyone ever asking me what I wanted, and if they did ask, I don't recall them ever offering to deliver what I wanted, if I'd known what I wanted. But I've never known what I've wanted. Not-want, you know, that's more a problem in our society than money-mad criminals, or lazy drug addicts. They, and the prostitutes, and the wretched filth everyone needs to prosecute, they suffer from not-want, as in I do not want to work a demeaning job, or I do not want to live on the litterstrewn streets, or I do not want to live in the wretched past, or I do not want to try to be what I've never had the chance to be. I can hear Hog now, laughing, calling me a cheap philosopher. Stop thinking, stop thinking, he'd say, stop thinking and just breathe, and eat, and fuck—that's all we're meant to be, Bones. We breathe and we eat and, when we're really lucky, we fuck. Yes, we shit and talk and fight and many other things, but we can go a while without those things, but we need to breathe, eat, and fuck, else we die. So go fuck, Bones. Or go fuck yourself, if you have to...

Hog, of course, was the mastermind of our misadventure. That we let him lead us is perhaps a sad statement of our leadership abilities, but in the land of the blind the one with delusions of seeing is always king. Bejowled and pink-faced, short and curly red hair, a stocky man yet surprisingly agile, Hog was impossible to ignore. He wasn't exactly charismatic; he was more like a livid wart on a fashion model's face. In a crowd of beautiful people one's eyes would always be drawn to Hog. Plus, he had a shocking singing voice. Hog could be standing on your throat, cackling with laughter, and then break into song, high-pitched and wavering, something which would bring tears to your eyes, and then he'd crush your windpipe, or boot your testicles into a bleary tomorrow.

Him, Weasel would say, he ain't right. He's got the potential, you know? You see me pointing to my head, Bones? He's. Got. The. Potential. He could be, like, a singing waiter at some fancyshit five star, or in a movie. Singing! Fuck, he can dance. You see him bust those moves last week at Ye Old Bear? Fuck, Bones, I think Hog there takes pity on us, lowers himself to give us guidance. But a man like that, he's got the potential, he's got a higher ceiling, you know? I think we should both go and kiss his rosy ass right now. Because him, he's meant for better things than the likes of us. See, me? Me? I ain't got the potential. I'll admit it. Sure, everybody says I have skills, tricky hands, now you see your wallet, now you don't. But fuck, Bones, I've given it lots of thought, and it's just because I'm too stupid to know what fear is. I reach and grab and I run before I can even think of reaching and grabbing and running. I'm an idiot. I ain't got the potential for more than that. You ever hear me try to sing, eh? You don't want to hear me sing, Bones. That's a horror show right there, that is. That's a horror show. You won't sleep for weeks.

Weasel I always got on best with, because there were no ugly surprises with Weasel. If you could get past the wretched state of his teeth, his sour breath, you could sit for hours and listen to Weasel. He said he knew nothing about nothing but never lacked an opinion. I don't know about the state of the shitty world, Bones, but I'm pretty fucking certain everyone's been bitching about the cancerous decline of it for centuries. Them butt-loving Greeks and Romans, them fucking Israelites and other ancient royal shitheads, no doubt in my mind they were talking about crazy kids and criminals and corruption and what the fuck. You know? Yet here we are, Bones, still breathing the air, still drinking our minds numb, still trying to give a fuck. But what do I know?

It's really too bad, because Weasel was the one with the potential. Didn't even have a criminal record. A dozen years of charmed existence. Whereas Goose, Goose was the worst kind of foul, someone you could never get to know because he was the reflection, or maybe the shadow. He was who he needed to be to gain your trust. He'd sit and listen and you'd forget he was there with you, except he'd make that sound in his throat, which is why we called him Goose, and his long neck, and the more you looked at him the more you could picture a beak, or a bill, whatever geese have. He said he wasn't always aware of the sound he was making, a small honk, a nervous thing, allergies, just said there was a tickle sometimes. Hog: Could you stop making honk, Goose? Could you just stop for a minute, while we try to think? No more honk. Say no to honk! I have had my fill of honk today, Goose! Leave!

Goose would leave, too. Go outside for a smoke or sit expressionless at the bar. When he'd return we'd hardly notice, until the tick-honk was heard during a quiet, pensive moment.

\*

So here's the scene. It's evening and we meet at Froggies. Hog herds us into a corner booth, telling the elderly couple sitting behind us about the poor soul who went into convulsions just days ago, blood gushing from all nine holes, squirting on the walls and all over the table, a horrible, horrible death, saying how brave it was of them to sit there and eat the fish, to look gruesome death in the oozy eyesocket, and of course the troubled sweet couple move on and we have the corner to ourselves. Later the manager will come have a word with us, and Hog will buy drinks for everyone, if only to stress the point he's made at this little meeting, but I'm getting ahead of myself.

"Well, me fellow arsehearts," says Hog, "we've got ourselves a wee predicament, don't we? Nod yes, me arsehearts. Good boys. Seeing that none of us are exactly highly employable, we sometimes find ourselves a little short of cash, right?"

"Just picked a pocket," says Weasel. "Third one this week."

"And you're rich now, are you? No, you're not rich, Weasel, and you will never be rich, Weasel."

"Don't wanna be bloody fuckin' rich, Hog. Just want food, a bed, beer, and women… a motorcycle would be nice…"

"How about a place with a steaming Jacuzzi, eh?"

"Oh fuck yeah, gotta sit those women somewhere…"

"And that convertible," Goose puts in, "you're always going on about it."

"Oh yeah, fuck! Fuck, put the Jacuzzi in the convertible. Jesus."

"So, Weasel, arsehole of my heart," says Hog, "you want to be rich."

"Well, fuck… but not too rich, huh? They're all queers, wearing white, as if money makes them holy and pure."

"You worry about being pure, Weasel?"

"Oh I do, Bones. Me and purity? It's an ugly date."

"Who else wants more money?" Hog points to each of us. We shrug.

"So we're all a-fucking-greed, then? We're for more money?"

Yes. Sure. Uh huh.

Weasel, the pick pocket extraordinaire, Goose the kind to jump you in an alley, take your wallet, your girl, and your leather shoes—and me, I tended toward fraud, little schemes to draw people in with the promise of more money. I had an honest face. I still do. Sometimes I believed in the fraud, believed in the power of spreading hope, even if the results always came up short. Told an old lady once, a rich old lady, near death and with no heirs, told her I was a long lost nephew. You look just like my dear ex husband, she quavered. Ended up holding hands on her deathbed, giving most of her money to cat charities, weeping for weeks.... Hog? Hog robbed two banks in his youth, made out like the bandit he was on the first, got nabbed on the second, spent some time behind real fucking bars, but said he was always willing to trade two years of high living for ten years in prison, because without the high living it's all pretty much prison anyway.

"Right, me arsehearts?"

He takes a paper place-mat and, as our drinks arrive, draws a dozen little money signs around the edges "for inspiration." He then draws a diamond in the centre, and Weasel is impressed: "Ahh, good fuckin' diamond, man. I can't draw for shit." He then draws us as stick figures and writes our names over each and gives us second names: Goose is The Beggar, Weasel is The Hider, Hog is The Hammer, and Bones is The Nice Customer. I don't like The Nice Customer, but I don't say anything. Once again, my honest face getting in the way of real excitement.

"The plan," says Hog, "is to steal some pretty diamonds. Why diamonds? Well, me hardy arsehearts, because diamonds are what's called easily potable; put them in your pockets, your ears, shove them up your doodah. You don't need a getaway van and three fools—no offenses, brothers—lugging a safe. You don't need a room in a warehouse to store them. Jesus, no one ever finds diamonds again. They vanish, poof! They're not stamped with serial numbers. They don't slip out of their ropes and squeal to the police. They just shine."

"And fuck, think about it," Weasel whispers, "they're just rocks pulled from the dirt. A fucking worm crawling through the fucking mud wouldn't give a rat's ass about a shiny rock. It's just us crazy fuckers. And hell, nothing shines in the mud."

"Exactly," says Hog. "We ain't stealing Mama's kidneys like fuckface there."

"Alisdair Squidley," I say.

"Nobody's going to miss these diamonds, is the point," says Hog.

"What about the diamonds' owners?" says Goose, from the dark.

"Who the fuck cares, Goose? People who have diamonds can always get more diamonds," says Hog.

"But I'm thinking they will miss them a bit, Hog," says Weasel.

"OK, arseholes, after the heist we will send

them a get well soon card. That better?"

"That's classic, Hog, utterly fucking classic."

We all agreed to send it and sign it, the card, but then change our minds.

Hog begins to outline the plan, starting with the location of the jeweller, The Carat Top, the day of the heist, the time, what we should be wearing to fit our profiles (he has cut images from magazines), our budget for purchasing those items (money for all except Goose, who's told to dig through the trash to find what he needs), the need for receipts (you arses aren't ripping me off), and the where and whens of our practice runs. Hog is a firm believer in perfection through repetition, says actors, musicians, dancers, athletes, they all practice, but thieves? Most are too stupid to practice, and they wonder why they get caught! Meanwhile, the television has caught my eye, the Prime Minister telling the Nation's Joke of the Day, something about a large fish and midget lawyer in a Turkish bathhouse, something about there being only one towel, and Hog snaps his stubby pink fingers in my face.

"A clean shirt, Bones! You'll need a clean white shirt, and maybe a tie. Do you have an iron? Does anyone here have an iron?" Goose raises his hand. I tell Hog that I hate goddamn ties and can't I just be a nice customer without one? I'd be an upstanding citizen if the tie had never been invented. "You need a tie, Bones," Hog says, "because you're a religious fucking nutcase, a slickhaired sincere sucker of God's righteous toe, OK? You'll have to have them totally distracted, entranced, flustered and…"

"Confused!" Weasel shouts. "Oh it's classic, Hog, they'll be like, he was so religious, and jolly God was in the room, and then they started stealing our bloody diamonds, and at first we thought it was a good thing, but then we didn't, wah wah wah."

"And you have to be believable, Bones."

Well, it seemed a reasonable plan and I was willing to go along with it, but if you'd asked me if I believed it would work I would have told you no, probably not, we'll all end up in jail because something will go wrong. But no one asked me that, and so I never thought about it.

At the end of the night, after the manager spoke to us, Hog took what Weasel had stolen, paid for everyone's drinks and made a singing apology, danced on a table and jumped into Goose's waiting arms. The seven or eight patrons applauded for a few seconds. The manager shook his head and told us to fuck off into the dark. That's what we did, crashing at Hog's mother's place.

*Sweet Mother of Hog*

The next few days went quickly enough, as much as I remember, because every night would end with the four of us soused at Froggies or some other pub. Hog had given us two weeks to be ready for the heist, to get our acts together, and so I set about trying to find a clean white shirt with a collar for a goddamned tie, which turned out to be harder than you would think in our part of town. Weasel and I first checked clotheslines, but the only clean white collared shirt we found was hanging from a fourth story balcony. Eventually we walked into a used clothing store and the manager, a tall bald woman who perhaps used to be a homely man, did find us a shirt, in fact several of them, though all were too big and the one that did fit was more pink than white (salmon, said Weasel, laughing, it's salmon!) and what the fuck, I took it. And a tie, too. Black.

"Classic! Nothing says religious fucking nutbar like a salmon shirt with a tie, Bones. Classic."

"You sure it's not too girly, Weasel?"

"Nah, Hog'll love it. You're going the extra mile, Bones. Takes a big man to do that, right? Hey, there's Goosey."

Down an alley Goose came toward us carrying a bundle of the filthiest set of rags one would never want to imagine. The sour reached us long before Goose got within chatting distance.

"Jesus, Goose," I said, "wear those and you won't need a weapon."

"Excuse me kind sirs whilst I vomit," said Weasel, who pretended to stagger.

Goose looked pleased with himself, was sporting a welt over his left eye and scratches on his cheek. Story goes he was approaching one bum wondering how to negotiate the removal of the bum's clothing, which would most likely have been done with a few swift kicks, when another bum jumped him from behind. "Fell on my face, he said, "'cuz he'd grabbed my arms, you're pretty much fucked when someone does that. And when someone does that to me they're pretty much fucked, too.

"Hey, Bones… think Hog will mind if I wash them?"

"Which fine set are you going wear, Goose?" said Weasel.

"I was thinking of mixing and matching, maybe."

"Ah, fuck yeah. Good idea, Goosey."

"The stink has to be authentic, Goose."

"Oh yeah, Goose, I mean it would take you what? At least a week before you could make them really stink again."

"Sure. Right. But I'm keeping my own clothes underneath."

"I don't know, Goose, gonna be pretty hot under there. Me, Goose,"—and here Weasel opened his vest, showing his white tee—"I like to go light. Keeps me cool, because sweating isn't where it's at for pick pockets, and neither are jackets full of pockets, because once someone looks around and sees ya, they see what? They see me, practically naked, nothing more innocent than that, and smelling good, too."

"But," I said, "he's a bum, Weasel. Bums do like the layered look."

"Oh well but I wouldn't do it. I'm just saying."

"So," said Goose, "are you going nude then?"

"Wha?"

"Mister Invisible, right?"

"Nah, not nude man!"

"Why not? Can't say there's a whole lot to see."

"Yeah, but them jewellers are used to squinting, Goose," I said

"Ah fuck both of ya. I can do invisible in my sleep. I can do invisible while screaming in a church.

I am invisibility incarcerate, dinkheads."

"Incarcinate, listen to him."

"Honk honk honk, listen to you!"

And while Goose and Weasel wrestled themselves to the sidewalk, I went over my role in my head, what I would say, the posture I would use, maybe an accent, too? What religion would I be? One I liked, or one I disliked? Did any religion fit either of those categories? It would have to be one I liked because pretending to like something you detest, well it always comes across as phony. They'd become suspicious. Hey, see his eye twitch when he said NeoBaptist? They'd spot Weasel. Goose wouldn't stink enough, and next thing the alarm is ringing and four out-of-shape beery losers are fleeing the scene. So I would have to be sincere. But what did I believe in?

Hi, I'm Charlie Fink from the Church of Some False Hope. Yes, just another salesman for eternal fraud...

I also went through the twistings and turnings of the tie. Something about a fox chasing a rabbit down a hole. Was that it? Swinging around a mulberry bush?

Maybe Hog would know.

*

It was dusk when we arrived at Ye Old Bear, the neon green Beer Bear flickering and a crowd gathered on the patio. We waited for Hog. Wasn't like him to be late. Weasel wondered if something had happened to Hog, was saying, "Shit, man, not to Hog," and wondering if the cops had caught on to us, had decided to chop off the head, make us run around like blind fucking squirrels falling out of trees. "We are fucked if they got him, Bones. "

I took a sip, said, "Should we promote from within, or hire out?"

"Jesus fucking Christ, Bones, no offense but none of us are leadership material. I would piss everybody off, Goose would beat everybody up, and you just don't care enough…"

"Hey now…"

"… about money to lead us anywhere but the poorhouse."

"So we should post an ad, huh?"

"Yeah, yeah… fuck. Marginally ambitious fellows looking for event planner. Must have verbal skills and bulk. Singing is a plus. And…"

"Do not come with mother in tow."

And cue Hog entering with a stooped ogress hooked on his arm. Mother hasn't been with Hog in some time, but here she is, her red hair as wild as the wind, her make up smeared and lips baboon like, though at the moment I couldn't tell you what a baboon's lips look like. It's misaligned lipstick. Her face is slack. "Shit," says Weasel. I ask Hog if the nurse has run out again and Hog's mother mutters "Filthy fucker," not slurred at all. "Found her next door staring in the neighbour's goddamn bedroom window," Hog says quietly, "watching them hump like dogs, and said, 'Mamma, why you wanna watch that?' And she says, 'Oh it's very old, you know.' 'What's old?' I say to her, and she just pats me on head. Jesus. We do this right, guys, and I'm locking her up."

Then Hog made it clear that that was all for the night. Mother would repeat everything to everyone and to the stray cats and birds as well. And she would say it in haunting ways. Singsong. My son the thief is illicit in the night, Luv, she'd say. Or the black wings of fever have taken the boys to the blood of the diamond. Her nurses, Hog once explained, leave because she messes with their heads.

So we talked of inconsequentials. Goose honked off early and Weasel and Hog got deep into a conversation about the freakiness of reality, with Mother occasionally joining in. Myself, I wandered inside, sat, focused on the television. Beer commercials. Sports highlights. And then Moll again, in the news. An activist group claiming to have an exclusive interview with Moll the Pig. A woman has entered the farm, no, has penetrated the prison, she's tall, dark-haired and moving stealthily, dressed in black like the others in her group. It's night and lights flash amidst the stalls in a barn. They hide. They move from stall to stall. And then… *is that the scar?* The screen shows Moll the Pig after the Operation, then the pig on the screen. Diagrams show that it's the same scar. Quick. Floodlights and the pig blinks blindly, retreats to a corner. The woman jumps in and asks the pig if he's Moll, is he the accused mass-murderer Moll? The pig looks left, right, appears the jostle the camera, oh it's trying to escape the stall, ramming the gate, but the woman is still in there, in the shit and slop, are you Moll, are you Sylvester Moll? Grunt or squeal if you can! She's knocked over, the pig is above her. Leering. Straddling her with its big pink pig body, the scar pulsing, and then squealing, squealing in rage, or anguish. Or just squealing. The screen goes black.

*Sheep on the Lam*

I will not lie and tell you my little legs flew, that once far from my prison I leaped high fences and bounded through meadows, revelling in my freedom. The sun had vanished and the sky had turned a dark grey, like wet wool, and the instinct to turn back was always there. But instinct isn't the right word. More an impulse, or a compulsion. Returning was right, leaving was wrong.

Bad, bad sheep.

Panic set in. My legs shook. I stopped in a huddle of trees, trying to catch my breath. Fuck, I thought, I'm in a sheep's body and men sheer sheep and eat sheep and shit and why aren't they following me? Oh, I must be tagged. But where? I rubbed up against a tree trunk, rolled on the ground, stuck out each leg and shook it hard. I had skinny black legs. Dammit. Should I disguise myself? How do I do that? Dark glasses? A hat? A raincoat? What the hell am I supposed to do? I need to get to a phone, yes… What was her name? A bird. She would help me, she had tried before, during the trial, in the hospital. Right, right.

But that didn't go well.

And would she recognize my voice?

Did I have a voice?

With little other choice, I started to run again, and it was easier going down the hill. I decided to let my body move the way it knew to move, and to not fight it, because when I fought it I felt like I was being carried along, as if my neck was an arm and my head held out at the end of the neck-arm. And as I was running down the hill to who knows where I flashed back to the talk of surgery, the oh-fuck-ness of that, how the eyes and the nerves had to be stretched to fit the pig's wide-set eye sockets and how that would be even more extreme in cows and yes, sheep. *These braincases aren't meant for this, so it takes some trickery*, said the doctor and I was close to stumbling from thinking. We really don't know the longterm effects of conforming the human brain into these confined spaces. We have drugs that do shrink the brain, but the criminal, or should I say *Constock*, will likely suffer an endless headache. Perhaps this is part of the punishment?

My head didn't hurt. At least I didn't think it hurt. Maybe it's been hurting all along and headaches are a human luxury? With a headache we can beg off anything. I slowed at the bottom of the hill where there was a brook and then started to drink like the animal I mostly was, no thoughts of *e. coli* or pesticide run-off and as I got close to the water I saw the orange collar around my neck. Now, as a sheep, the collar was just a thing, as many things are just a thing and you never give a thought to things. Cars and helicopters and ringing phones and lawn mowers are just things and it does a sheep no good to think of things. Yes, there's a part of the sheep brain, I've observed, that wants to know, but there's a wall, or perhaps it's like a bright fruit so high in a tree and no matter how hard you leap you can't get it. Sheep just don't get it. If they had a little more grey matter they'd climb atop one another, form a woolly pyramid and taste the fruit…

But they don't.

I was drinking and wondering how to remove the collar when I heard a dog bark. My legs straightened and my head jerked high. How many dogs? Sounded like only one dog. Can I outrun a dog? Images of dogs chasing sheep. Probably not. So I leaped across the brook and tried to see where the dog was coming from, saw that it was coming down the hill I had just come down. Were there others? People? No. Just the black dog. OK, once the dog got close to the brook, either leaped or scramble-swam through the water, I'd leap back across. Then it would do the same. It could go on forever. But the dog would bark more and more. Others would come. Well at least it wasn't a mean dog, and was, I could now see, a border collie. So it wouldn't attack me.

I let the dog come across the brook (it hesitated, then jumped), and decided to act casual, which wasn't easy because a very jerky part of me viewed the dog as some kind of greater power. A fucking dog. The dog barked and looked at me, curious, perhaps trying to recognize me. I could see the wheels turning, turning, and then he barked some more, made a move to nip at one of my legs and I turned to face him. His head tilted. Yeah, I'm not your normal sheep, asshole. I can predict everything you do. The dog turned quickly, looked back over the hill. Oh, you have a flock back there, don't you? And you're worried about them? It's a dilemma, isn't it? The dog barked.

You come! You... come! Uh... come!

Well that's how I interpreted it, and you know, following him started to make a lot of sense. I had this orange collar around my neck. As a running sheep I was a sitting duck. But a flock, yes, I could hide in a flock. I made what I hoped was a passable sheep sound and followed the dog. It felt good to let him lead me. My flock awaited but could the dog just let it be? Could we simply trot side by side and the dog not get fucking annoyed? I mean, I'd stop a second, just to get my bearings, where was the farm I left, where were we going, where was the city, catch my breath, and the dog would freak. You have an overdeveloped sense of superiority, yet mixed with deep insecurity, I wanted to tell him.

From the hilltop I saw the city below the ragged clouds, saw smokestacks and distant glinting of cars when the sun would shine for a moment. I wondered if I could make it to the city in one day, but that seemed unlikely seeing I was now heading back the way I came. The dog circled and barked, crouched before me, circled, made to bite again, so I moved along. And moving along felt good, and those nips made my hindquarters twitch, but still, every now and then I'd stop just to piss the dog off. Ah, and then I heard the sheep, a multitude of wonderful, self-same, unsheered sheep. The welcoming woolly masses. How easy it is to simply be.

\*

Let me clear up a few things before judgement sets in. I say I am a man in a sheep's body, but is that entirely true? I breathe into a sheep's lungs, and sheep's blood flows through my sheep's heart. I eat sheep food and shit sheep shit. My hormones are a mixture of man and sheep. If it's odd to desire stocky little ewes, must I point out that men without the sheep admixture have desired a little ewe here and there and who can say what impure thoughts sheep have had over the centuries? I saw how they looked at the farmer's wife's bottom and the farmer's swinging sex in his baggy trousers. We've seen sexual response from dogs and dolphins, rabbits and chickens, chimps and sea lions. Desire, I say, knows no bounds.

Limitations, yes.

For example: I did not want to take any particular ewe out to dinner, or buy her roses. I did not want to run along the beach with her or melt hot wax on her several nipples. And though I have a delectable thing for garters, a ewe's thigh inspires only hunger of another sort. And that, too, is a bothersome feeling. Hunger also knows no bounds.

Furthermore, it is obvious that when men have no otherwise normal release, they will attempt to mate with pretty much anything around. In prisons, it's other men, ones for whom they'd not bat a single eyelash on the outside. In furniture warehouses, it's the soft creases of plush chesterfields. When lost at sea in a boat, alone, the gannet and the sea otter suffice, though holding them still often proves a challenge. I once had a roommate who did unspeakable things to a vat of lard. Need I go on?

In any case, I was amongst my kind, my shadow and their shadows were the same shadow. And I had just started to relax, just started to nuzzle up to a young ewe in perhaps her first heat, so sweetly nibbling grass, had just started to breathe in her heavenly ewe-scent, had just started to lose myself in heady sheepness when that damn border collie nipped my leg and, I swear, gestured to the barn. Was that a head toss, puppy? What's in the barn, huh? Well, I'm busy here, can't you see?

I ignored the dog, who I decided to call Jack, and returned to the ewe, who I decided to call Jill, and I heard Jack run off and Jill, now facing me with a curl of grass hanging from her uh, lips, she seemed to sigh, then look shyly away. Oh, such a tease. I followed her to the crest of the hill, stood next to her, saw the creek far below, the city farther, saw no sign of my prison and felt the sleepy pull of sheepness. Then a goat-like cloud blocked the sun, made a goat sound and the horizon became the sky, the sun a ringing mountain of wheeling stars.

## Moll's Shaggy Minions

I woke with the worst headache. I moaned deep in my throat, tried to plant the palm of my hand on my forehead, then rub my temples. My arms didn't move that way. I struggled to get up, get four square beneath me and face my captors, who were facing me: face of a dog, face of a goat. The barn went boaty and I stumbled into the wall. Where was my brain, dammit?

From the floor I saw that the orange collar had been removed. Chewed. The goat head-gestured and the dog—Jack—pounced on the collar and ran off, darted through the barely-open door and it was me and the pale goat and the brown barnlight.

You're a fucking ugly goat, you know? And how the hell did you get me in here? I looked at my left side, which was filthy... and yes, my back legs hurt. Dragged me, huh? Nice. The goat, who needed an ugly name to match his ugly face, but hell if I could think of one at the moment, came over and forced my head to the floor, seemed to be checking the back of my skull, and when he pulled back, I swear he, it, was smiling.

So what's going on here? How about you show

me yours too, Fergus? Fergus, yes, that's a name for you. Are you Constock, Fergus? I got to my feet, tried to circle around, see the back of Fergus's head, but he was having none of it. He was mostly white, had floppy ears, small pink eyes. You're a fucking failure, Fergus. Before they made you a goat, you were a... what? A goat-fucker? Life sentence for the goat-fucking boy, was that it? Hell, why not experiment on the abomination! Do you know how much my head hurts right now? No, I don't think you do, you don't have that spark that I saw in Moll's little pig eyes... there's no humour there.

Fergus, not giving up any secrets, brought me a dish of sweet oats, plus a bowl of water, and I desperately needed both. The part of me that eats, and I don't mean mouth, I mean that automatic gulp-it-down, it simply leaps into action. And food isn't so much a pleasure, but a need, like voiding your bowels. You do it. And you watch, you always watch. The wolf is in every shadow; every flash in the dark is his eyes. The wolf burrows underground and falls from clouds. I still have dreams, yes, of gnawing a tough weed, pulling and pulling and great sheep god in heaven, I pull out a wolf. It ravages my belly.

After a while Jack returned and guarded the barn door. Fergus paced back and forth, and Jack watched that too. I did wonder if I could slip past Jack, slip out into the night, overcome that awesome fear and run, run. Maybe I could have done that, but I wasn't exactly being mistreated, and it's very sheep to be content when your life is out of your hands, or hooves. Hooves! I trotted up to Fergus, tapped a hoof on the barn floor and scratched two words in the soil: *how long?* It was hell to do it, friends, pure hell and I don't know why. It was torture to write, as if part of me recoiled from words, from abstraction, and it wasn't getting through to Fergus either, who'd look to floor, nibble a piece of hay that was on the word "long," look back at me. I mean, maybe Fergus was Icelandic, or spoke Swahili, or was illiterate, or was just a fucking ugly goat. I dabbed at the words with my hooves, over and over, How long, Fergus? How long will you hold me here? How long before a farmer or a prison guard comes through that door? How long till the end of the Universe? How long? How long?

But nothing, not even a scratch, a squiggle. And Jack was agitated. OK, puppy, I'll rest now. We'll all sleep a while. We'll all twitch and shudder in this old barn, while my stomachs rumble and I fart, while my woolly hide itches and my eyes look down on the horror that is my muzzle. There's a smiling scar on the back of my head, I know it's there, feel it throb, it's a crescent moon that I can't leap as children in their sick beds count, count, count until sleep enshrouds them. They don't see the wolf in pursuit of the leaping sheep sighing on the floor of a barn on a hill, stars wheeling overhead the insane city where Hog and his hounds fuck prison-rate clowns and Weasel snaps bedbugs between his teeth, and Robyn, yes, that was her name, remember me, remember she said, removing her wings, her bird mask in the stairwell, remember that we tried, remember who you are, remember that you are innocent and the bastards, the bastards, ah look at how fucked I am, pretty fucking funny, isn't it? I stretched out, tried to get comfortable but it wasn't happening, I'd long been an insomniac and I hadn't realized how much that had changed the last few months, but then again I hadn't realized much the last few months. Fergus and Jack were lying somewhere in the dark, I could hear but not see them, and I recalled the doctors telling me they'd leave my human eyes, you'll be a blue-eyed sheep, ha ha, sure to get lots of dates, ha ha, oh sweetie, ha ha, but seriously, sheep vision sucks and there'd be body-brain conflict and the program is meant to be just, but not cruel.

Well, sorta cruel.

Murderers.

So much was going through my head, the past, the future, and suddenly grief, but big sheep don't cry. I closed my eyes and didn't dream of wolves. My mind wandered further and I recalled the news of the first attempt, a deranged Bonobo named Kiki, brain slapped into the hollow of a llama, what could be more docile than a llama? And Kikillama sending the camera-carrying doctors scrambling into a van, Kikillama smashing feet through the windshield, going for their throats... And someone in the van shrieking *Hindbrain, you removed the hindbrain, you fucking morons, you removed...*

Hog, the day before the heist, finally asking me why I was called Bones, "I mean it's not as if you're all skin-and-bones." And telling him I used to be, was nothing but, and Hog nodding, pasting pictures of the gang onto a bristol-board drawing of the jewelry store, not knowing I was lying, that when I was a boy I'd wanted to be doctor, because doctors had nice houses and got to see girls' privates and no one let me forget it, and isn't it ironic? That's what you get for not following your dreams, and let that be a lesson to you, boys and girls.

Sleep, if sleep comes, it comes like lead on your

head, crushing consciousness, so you stay awake.

\*

And from one state of wakefulness you enter another, see the barn door moving, cracked open, see Fergus pacing about nervously in the light from the morning sun. You smell the dew and think fuck some fresh grass and a good shit would be sweet right now but things are ahoof, Jack comes racing in, Jack is all excited, sticks his eager nose into all corners of the barn, returns to the door and barks once.

I hear a pig grunt.

Well, if I hadn't been in full Bones-brain, I was now. Jesus Christ that sounded like a very large pig. That sounded like a pig-grunt from the bowels of pig Hades. What the fuck were the doctors thinking? Pigs and men, men and pigs—there's not enough separation.

A chicken entered the barn, and then another. Then Jack, who I swear bowed his head as the pig entered. Except that, without my exceptional sense of smell, and the pig's exceptional smell, I wouldn't have known it was a pig, because its pig body was covered by black canvas... though it was pig shaped, yes, and there was the grunt, and now, I could see, a curly tail poking through, and those eyes...

Flashback to Ye Old Bear, the television, stills of Sylvester Moll; the eyes move closer, you think they're black but they're not, just a very dark brown, and you think he's laughing, but he's not.

Two more chickens pushed the door shut and it was me, Jack the Border Collie, two chickens, Moll the Pig, two more chickens, and Fergus, the ugly fucking goat.

I made a sheep sound and decided, I guess, to shit on the floor.


*Pearls Before Swine*

"So the most utterly important thing, Mates of Mayhem," says Hog, "is that we know our shit better than they know their shit. They will look for clues. Hide your fingerprints with nice soft gloves? Well gloves have fingerprints, too. *Fibre* prints. Burn your prints away? Smudges have lumps of DNA. Touch nothing? They will sniff the air for your farts and they will be able to tell from what market and on what day you bought that broccoli. So you're fucked. And cameras"—points to the high corners of the room—"are everywhere..."

"Nah, don't like it," says Weasel, sitting in the back, arms crossed. "You know why? It spells MOM! We can't be known as the *MOMs*, Hog, that ain't gonna cut it!"

Hog bends, rises, throws a shoe at Weasel, then Goose complains that it's his shoe, and here we are, in Hog's mother's basement, which has been set up with cardboard boxes to mimic the ill-fated jewelry store, right down to the sale signs and sections highlighting the best stuff, the highly potables, as Hog says. Two manikins stolen from Die Vest, a high-end German clothier where Hog used to work, stand stolidly behind the cardboard countertops. A large white bra wraps the torso of one, a gun-shaped penis is drawn on the torso of the other. Mother continually pounds on the door at the top of the stairs.

"Pay a-fucking-tention, OK? Why in the withering world is that so fucking hard for you fuck-ups? *Hey, we're fuck-ups, that's why*," says Hog in a demented voice. "And we just want to go out and play in the sun, yippee, hooray." Hog dances on his toes, does some kind of ballet spin, kicks a box across the room and shouts at his mother to just fucking croak already. Mother screams through the door, "The animals are lichen! Animals! Lichen!"

"I think she wants her bra back," says Weasel.

Hog puts his hands on his head, sits on a box chair, which creaks, collapses.

Well, this wasn't how it was supposed to go.

See, we were going to do it right, leave no shiny rock unturned. Hog had come up with a playbook called "The 50 Scenarios" and we'd practice five a day for ten days and it was, in Weasel's words, "Einsteinian in its brilliance, fucking Einsteinian, like Hog equals em-cee squared, you know? Where em is mucho and cee is currency." This was going to be the smoothest heist ever, this was going to be the opera, or some other really smooth stuff. "Other gangs," said Hog, "they'll whisper, they'll say who did it? Who are they? Rumours will fly, jewellers will shit themselves, the police will scratch their stubbly chins and eventually we'll just have to enter a joint, politely say we're the ones, and they'll swoon, hand over the money..."

"... ask for our fucking autographs, ha..."

"... and yes, ask for our fucking autographs."

It was what you could call the grandeur of delusions, if you wanted to call it something fancy and not something a little more sane, like a gang of cockeyed followers and a semi-psychopathic leader. We can't get past the first scenario—hell, we can't get past the introduction to the first scenario. Hog is near tears. I can hear Weasel rubbing his hands together. Goose is honking softly. Mother is perhaps singing, or flinging, scat. I stand, grab Hog's playbook from the cardboard counter-top, and read scenario one.

Scenario One: *So in scenario one me arsehearts, we four have entered The Carat Top and while Bones there chats it up about Godliness and Soap Weasel and Goose move ~~stelthily~~ quietly to each side of the counter whilst I engage Missus Carat Top using my captavating ways. Oh but then I notice a problem and I need to signal me arsehearts so I start to sing Danny Boy which means change in plans because I notice Missus CT has a big bulge in her throat and is in fact ~~violah~~ bingo Mister Carat Top in disguise and packing serious heat! So in this scenario the Missus and the Mister have worn each others clothing and what should we do about it?*

I repeat the scenario to Goose and Weasel and they shrug, look to Hog, but Hog is still prone on the floor, hands rubbing his temples. "So we're sure he'll be armed?" I say to no one in particular. "Dirty Dog Pound," says Hog from the floor, "shot in the abdomen after grabbing a silver pearl choker, half his bowel removed and shitting through a hose now." "Ha, shitting through his hose, Hog, that's sick," says Weasel. "D-Dog, you know, he wasn't one to plan things out, being a crackhead and all." "So what we do," says Goose, "is shoot them first, both of them, right between the eyes, and shoot the cameras, and shoot fucking pedestrians with their fucking baby strollers, and shoot the pigs when they come, and keep shooting 'til there's no one else fucking up our scenarios. How's that, Hog?"

Hog raises his arm, thumbs up. "You'll be carrying the guns and ammo, Goose my sweetheart."

"A rocket launcher, too," says Weasel, "in case of freaky helicopters."

"Write it down, Bones, write it all under Goose's Bloody Playbook, Rule One: Shoot everything, then die. After that write ditto-fucking-ditto forty-nine times then draw a picture of Mother Goose getting buggered in prison."

"Ha! Goose getting goosed, whoo, that's good, Hog."

By the end of the afternoon we have gone through three further scenarios, coming up with three equally useless responses, and then decide to head over to Froggies. At Froggies Hog fills his mother's pockets full of coins, sits her at a lottery terminal, tells her to win herself a one-way trip to heaven and returns with, yes, beer. Goose though, from the moment we sit, starts to get on Hog, saying we can do it now, we can just go the fuck over and do it *now*, smash the door, grab the shit and run. Hog listens, says nothing, while I sit lower in my chair wanting to slip out through the floor, slip deep down into the earth and start anew, rise up all phoenix like and come out clean, or at the very least find a better gang of hardy arsehearts.

Goose: I think you're scared, Hog.

Hog: (raises eyebrows)

Goose: (shrugs shoulders)

Hog: (tilts head slowly)

Goose: Let's do it now, tonight.

Hog: (Sighs)

Goose: Fifty fucking scenarios for one fucking reality!

Hog: Which is, my dear?

Goose: We point guns, they cower, we take jewels.

Weasel: Aw, man, chill will ya? Enjoy the beer, Goosey. And come on, that one where Missus gets naked in the safe room and tries to seduce us all? And Hog pushing the fucking dummy on you? *Kiss me! Kiss me!* That was....

Goose: (shakes head)

Hog: Necessary! Your problem, Goose my love, is that you don't see it right, you don't see it as a dance. It's like when you get a woman, you just fuck her, over, done, slap it back in, zip up, leave, find another and do it all again. But that won't make the stars sing songs about her, Romeo. You have to use finesse, you have to play, and when you do that right, a woman, she's like your oyster.

Weasel: Ech!

Goose: We stealing pearls now, Hog?

Hog: We're robbing fate blind, lover. Because the ass-fucking world has told us we don't deserve shit, that we don't deserve to shit, that we don't even deserve to eat shit. And if you're not scared of that, my long-necked honey, if you're not scared becoming fate's shit...

Weasel: Some people's trying to eat here?

It's a fine defense by our leader, and we do not rush out into the stale night and throw our bodies against a thick plexiglass door for hours, but I do think Goose has gotten to Hog, because Hog once was like Goose and perhaps was getting soft, or at the very least fears getting soft, or fears being seen as soft. And sometime during the night Hog's eyes focus on me and he watches me watch the television, watch the latest Constock Watch, pundits pondering who would be next and trying to match criminal with animal, thumbs up or thumbs down, viewers calling and giving their opinion, and much laughter, Squidley the Kidney Thief oh he would make a good lemur, and the Prime Minister saying good night all with a joke about a petting zoo and a monkey and a cake and a file and recalling the early debate, not whether putting the brains of criminals into animals was ethical, but what the program should be called. Early on, Crainimals and Cranimals were the favourites, but also Crimcrams and Penitentacles were in the picture and the debate was hot, my friends. Convictory, cried those who wanted to put a positive spin on things, and Pig Penitents said all who thought souls were redeemable. Those were the good old days.

Mother's pockets have more coins than they can support. She waddles to our table, says, "Better the oily otter than the eyeless daughter," and laughs, laughs till her pants fall to her ankles, and laughs some more, laughs as we lead her home, cackling about the oily daughter, the legless diner, the diamond blubber and her son's jiggly jowls.

The next morning we do it all again, the

scenarios, the fucking around, the uselessness. But on day three we stop and Hog says we need to act, not playact. That isn't what we need, I am sure of it, but as we've been through already, knowing what anyone needs is not my strength.

## *Moll, in the Pink*

He was a fine, fine boy, a little given to chasing the cats and dogs around, ya know, and hanging them from trees by their tails. But that's a boy for ya, right? Oh no we didn't see the crazy stuff till later, when he was much older, eleven or twelve, when his playmates began to, well, disappear. But still, they were boys, playing with fire, and spears, and nail guns.

Yes, boys will be boys.

*But what was it that made him a 'fine, fine boy,' as you say?*

Oh you know, he was so sweet, would come by and have tea and cookies and talk about the human body, all the parts, and ya know he loved to talk about knives and had a fascination with my husband's—rest his soul—power tools.

*This made him a fine, fine boy?*

Oh yes, he was so polite.

Most polite boy I'd ever met.

I can tell ya, them boys aren't so polite these days.

Mothers just don't bring them up right.

*But, Sylvester... he was brought up... right?*

Well no I'm not saying that... murderin' ain't right... but I tell ya, someone taught him manners....

It's strange what comes back to you in a time of crisis: a memory of two widows having tea, chatting with an unseen reporter, and behind them through a window a brown field, winter is nearing, crows fly by the window... Hog is snapping his fingers in front of my face, Fergus is about to headbutt me again and Jack, irrepressible Jack, is bowing in front of me, but looking me in the eye, as if to say do this, do this, dumb sheep.

I curtsied.

And when I curtsied Moll the Pig let out a roar of a squeal or a squeal of a roar and the chickens clucked a riot and Fergus's legs locked and he flopped to his side and Jack, well Jack just kept showing me how to bow. The Big Pig is here, so bow sheep, bow, bow now. Sorry, Jack. A curtsy was going to have to do, not because I wasn't entirely sure how to make my sheep body bow, but because I remembered a few more things about Moll, pre-pig, remembered how he reacted to any signs of weakness, how it excited him, how begging and pleading only meant a drawn-out, wretched death. Also, I wanted to be able to defend myself, because if he came at me with all his swiny bulk I would... what? I would run, what else could I do? Uppercut to the throat? Spinning back-kick? A half-remembered submission lock? Naked snake hold? No, I would run around and around followed by a caped pig, a goat, a dog, chickens...

I made the sheep sound, and it was unconvincing, the sound of a sheep about to vomit, perhaps. Moll grunted. Somewhere behind him there was a cluck.

Moll lowered his head so that I could see his scar. I did the same.

I guess that was like a bow.

Animals on their own in a barn probably don't do this. Sheep, I know, do not plan ahead, they do not think—in fact their best defense is a blank mind. When they raise their heads to smell or hear if a predator is near, they're readying their brains for emptying so that when the time comes there will be room for one thought: run. Chickens are highly independent, bossy, and do not tolerate the rule of pigs. The sense of superiority in chickens is sadly at odds with their lot in life, but more than anything, chickens want order in the world, and want to be the ones to bring about that order. The chickens did not, thank fucking God, come forward and show their scars. And neither did Jack nor Fergus, which I found comforting.

So Moll had sway over the animals, and why did this not surprise me? He certainly had sway over people, especially children. Odd how intimidating chickens can be. Jack, I knew Jack, had known so many dogs like Jack, but the ancient eye of the chicken is frightening. We know death, it says, because we saw death by the billions. We saw death's head come flaming from the blackness. It threw fire. It killed our mothers and our fathers. The earth was ash. For a million years we hovered over the wasteland until the green returned. But one day the ash will return. We await it.

Moll, meanwhile, had cleared the room of his minions and stood before the barn door, morning sun through the slats slashing his canvas cape. His nose twitched and he searched the ground for a bite to eat, came up with a twig but did not chew it. Instead he started to rub one end of it in the dirt and though it took a minute to process it all, what with the hindbrain running interference, Moll was, of course, writing. And hell, he wasn't just writing, he was doing it upside down so I could read it, and, I have to say, in a lovely cursive script.

*You cannot run, little sheep. Join us.*

With my hoof I managed to scratch out a question mark.

*We are few, but we are strong. The world will be ours.*

I blinked, looked around—at the ceiling, the corners, anywhere but the pig's eyes. The question mark remained.

*We are tunnelling, little sheep. Come see our tunnel.*

I wanted to say, why tunnel when you can leap? But I realized pigs aren't much for leaping, much less flying. And the more I thought about it, the more I realized it was foolish to think I could simply run. Surely I *wasn't* the first Constock to leap a little fence. If I'd kept running, what would I have encountered? I hoofed-scratched *Wall?*

*The Constockade is vast, little sheep. The perimeter is patrolled by wolves. Their brains are the brains of prison guards paralyzed during the Riots. Join us.*

I nodded. Moll nodded. I nodded again. Seemed a pleasant enough fellow, and it only made you think about the media and how it distorts. Maybe all the shots of him, as a pig, charging gates, farmers, cows, clouds, and his attack on the reporter in his pen, maybe it was understandable. Sometimes it's easy to confuse fear with rage. In my case, no, but I'm a sheep and sheep don't do rage well. But a pig! Why put Moll in a pig? Because it's good publicity for the Program and what's good for the Program is good for the Prime Minister. Ah, fuck. What a mess. They'd debated castrating Moll as well, as a pig, this I recall, to keep him calm, keep everyone safe, should he escape, but that became absurd, this idea of a murderous porker stalking the alleyways, and comical were images of Moll humping sows, shuddering pig rapture on his pig face, snot flying from his snout, so it was decided to let him sow his wild oats, his domestic sows, and those who said *but his sperm, his sperm* soon shook their heads clear, for surely they didn't transfer *that*.

And that's the way it was. Let's laugh at crime, let's laugh at criminals. Let's film them, even, the mafia thug and his accomplices, Farm Daze, coming soon. Episode One: The Goatfather. But after a year the public began to lose interest and the filming was cancelled and the program itself was in danger of being axed, yes. Some argued that we were gaining valuable knowledge of the Brain Body Conflict and that there'd be potential breakthroughs for, say, paraplegics, but in the end another mass murderer danced onto the scene, sang his song, and then the prison riot, all this while I awaited trial hoping I'd gotten off the meat hook if things went poorly in the courts, which of course they didn't. And here I am, or was, following a pig in a cape out into the sun (chickens pushing each barn door open), flanked by Fergus and Jack and being led to an abandoned school bus in a field, the field full of grazing sheep, sheep that cleared a path for Moll and his minions, sheep that were soon running while Jack did what Jack does, circling and crouching and herding them out of sight.

Was there something the sheep should not see?

I know what you're thinking, because I'm thinking it too, but at the time I wasn't thinking at all. It was more like, Hey, I'm following Sylvester Moll, what would the gang say if they could see me now? You've done alright, Bones, they'd say, you've done earned the respect of the most horrific piece of flesh to trot the earth since... someone name another really crazy fucker? Weasel would shout out, that Roman creep Caligula! Whoo, he was a mad fucker. See his film? Goose would then pull out a gun and shoot Moll between his little black eyes and, with knife in hand, flip me over, slice me from throat to groin. Right, fuck the gang, fuck every one of them. That's what this is all about.

Get me out of here, Moll, and I will be your servant for life.

*Tunnellers*

If my life were a film and one were watching, say, from the worn wooden barstools at Ye Old Bear, the next section would be presented in split screen. On the left side, you would see a nervous, somewhat clumsy mid-sized sheep following a large, black-caped pig into a school bus. An ugly, floppy-eared goat is impatiently pushing at the sheep's ass and a border collie is speeding in from afar. The procession, once inside the bus, which is full of white chickens, their beaks pecking at what remains of the green seats' stuffing, will move down the aisle toward the back of the bus where there is no floor, only stairs leading down into the dark earth. Meanwhile, on the right side, in the bright pink hallway of a Play Prison, three men in yellow and red polka-dot coveralls are being handed bundles and papers, are being led out into a parking lot and into the midday sun where they stop, look around, smile and high-five one another. Clown number one, you notice, is Hog. Clown number two, well hey, that's Goose. And three? The beard doesn't fool you, the teeth give all away: it's Weasel.

Yes, my friends, just as I, Bones the Sheep, was about to descend deep into the earth beneath an abandoned school bus, my traitorous friends were being released from Play Prison, were changing out of their prison playsuits and were heading toward Froggies to celebrate, get drunk, get laid (unlikely), get arrested again, spend the night in city jail, all while making Bones jokes such as *I wonder if they allow him to have a baaaahth?*

No doubt I'd be doing the same were situations reversed, if it had been Goose left behind. I'd be making jokes about how odd it must be for Goose to have had his brain implanted into a freaking human being. Weasel would fall on his back laughing, slapping his thighs. But maybe Hog wouldn't laugh, maybe Hog would feel responsible, a failed leader, one who couldn't control his gang, one who messed up not once, not twice, but three times. Sure, Play Prison wasn't difficult, but it was demeaning, grown men made to act like cats one day, squirrels another, and now go gather your nuts, little squirrels, and now beg like a puppy. Goose refusing and having electrodes zap his mind honkless. They will not break me, I am mean, not cuddly. Crayon time did not soften me. Dunk the Clown Day did not teach me humility. I will not be reprogrammed, I will not be silly, I will not eat my puréed peas and carrots and cream and jello. Yes, well, Play Prison is for those who have a Chance, while Pay Prison is for the irredeemable. Is it Play or Pay, Mister... Goose, is it?

Goose, you knew, would not be around long.

Beneath the bus, down a stairway made by jittery monkeys which Moll, pink ass first, descended gracefully (and which I descended in face-first fashion, damn my little legs), and then along a tunnel following Moll and followed by Fergus and the chickens, we came to a larger, dimly lit room, a feeding station, I gathered, because there were rabbits feeding on piles of hay and grass. The light was coming in through small holes above, and the rabbits paid us no heed, simply raised their ears, peeked, and returned to their fuelling. Moll had moved on ahead and so I followed, the large room behind, the sudden commotion of a few randy rabbit bucks chasing chickens fading, and it was quiet for a spell, the pig trotting ahead, my poor brain seeing this dark, enclosed space as a metaphor, and then you could hear it, the digging sounds, the chewing sounds, could see nothing but dust for a while but then my eyes adjusted and there were three tiers of rabbits on benches, digging, biting roots, digging while a couple of badgers kicked the dirt behind them, and two more badgers came up the tunnel and kicked the dirt behind them, and so on. And one big badger nipped at the rabbits, and I saw fear as they clawed quickly, and as it got brighter at the end of the tunnel I could see the scar on the back of big badger's head, and how was that possible, why was it so bright?

Before I could do anything about it, sheep was in control and I was running into walls, running back past the feeding station, glimpsing rabbits humping chickens, and down the tunnel leaping badgers and knocking over goats and somewhere taking a wrong turn and finding myself in a square of some sort, open, but underground, but the sky above also a square, and why was this shape so horrifying? Because only men make squares, men had been here, men will lock you in their square, take your fur, take your babies, your ewes, men who had no respect for anything at all! If only they knew what sheep knew, if only they knew to quell the hatred and be one with the meadow but men had left the meadow long ago, pulled the trees around them and huddled inside with fire, and fire was no one's friend. Why did men trust fire?

For a long time, I was left alone in the square. When I was found by Fergus and Moll I'd had time to nap, to dream of a time where I was a sheep watching clouds lazily pass over the square, to dream of a time where I watched a small rabbit enter, study the sky, and, like a furry rocket, leap out to freedom. And when I woke I had time to gather my thoughts and form a plan of sorts, for I needed to get to the city and set things right, get there and clear my name, make the gang confess, somehow, and perhaps Moll would help me, or perhaps not. Knowing his history, the perhaps not was much more reasonable.

*You must eat, little sheep; tomorrow is a big day.*

I hoofed a question mark. Was getting better at it.

*You will see, little sheep.*

Fergus the ugly goat then got behind me, nudged me forward, and only as I was leaving did I sense something, smell something, yes, that made my fleece stand on end, but it was forgotten as soon as I was guided through the tunnels and reached the field, where I was escorted back to the barn by Jack, who seemed chatty, though without words. If he could talk he'd tell me about every thing he chased, and how fast he ran, and how amazing he was. I spent the night in the barn, watched over by Fergus, and recalling, just before falling asleep, that there'd been a monkey, one of those small, whiskered ones with fearful eyes, and that before Moll, before Kikillama, the monkey, who'd done no wrong, had just lived an innocent monkey life…

Weasel, in Froggies: Hey, whatever happened to that freakin' monkey badger?

Me: Couldn't have lived long.

Weasel: Madness, Bones, madness.

*In Which We are Stupid?*

I'm not sure when Hog started calling us his arsehearts, but it was early, and it did fit perfectly, that mixture of disgust and love. Well, maybe not love, but an amount of affection, certainly. One could point out that he had an amount of affection for his mother, too, yet talked endlessly of losing her somewhere. Still, she was often by his side. Psychologically I find this fascinating, that he would surround himself with things he wished to be rid of.

"Rise and grime, me arsehearts," says Hog. "Rise and slime! Rise and.... never mind! Get up, lazy fuckers!"

We are sleeping in the basement again, hungover, confused, falling out of waste-bin dreams and staggering to our feet. At one point during the night we'd trashed the cardboard mock-up, our practice site, which lead to someone crying. I looked around, trying to recall the grim weeper, had a flashback of Weasel sobbing, right, and a smashed-to-bits manikin, right, and Goose kicking and ripping and Hog drinking and singing and Weasel saying, I think I loved her, really really loved her and holding a plastic hand to his face, So soft, so ladylike.

I sat again and rubbed my temples, held down the urge to vomit and recalled rambling on about the winter of our discontent and deformities and Weasel saying, You're a playwright, man, a play writer, that's why you're so good at fraud, ya know, and right—then wondering if all writing was fraud, little schemes to keep us tricked into happiness, and Weasel saying, The Bible, man, that's the biggest fraud there ever was and Goose going nuts, right, it was all coming back.

And Hog is telling me, right there, right now, to

get up, to get the skillet hot and flip some pancakes. He throws me an apron.

"Breakfast, me arsehearts!"

And so begins the most fateful day of my life. We all head upstairs where mother, three bottles of vodka at her feet, snores away on the couch. Hog puts on some waltzy classical music, "Bay-fucking-toven," Weasel says, and out come the ingredients, the flour and the eggs, the butter and the buttermilk, salt and baking soda and "Paprika to give us verve," Hog says, and it's all done smoothly, no measuring cups, no fuss, quick whisking, and this, I'm thinking, it's what Hog could have been, a dancing singing breakfast chef, a man with charm, but you look to the couch and see Mother, and you recall the two or three stories of Father, and you know that some kids just never have a chance, that to be happy, or successful, to *try*, well it's a foreign thing and not welcome. It's a revelation, but I don't share it, the skillet is sizzling and the batter's being poured, yellow like the sun that's rising, yellow like Weasel's teeth or Goose's eyes, Goose who's fouling up the washroom, Weasel who's wondering what got up his nose ("I think it's a dime, man"), and Hog who seems content, but he's not humming along, he's lost in thought at the window. "Leave a few for

Mother, Bones," he says.

At the table we drink coffee, "Only the best coffee, freshly ground," Hog says, "stuff I've been saving for a special occasion, arsehearts, a bean grown in a lush valley in Kenya that gets exactly three hours of sunlight each day—you can fucking taste the mountain shadow, eh? And the maple syrup is a rare Maniwak blend, from maples whose branches have only known snow sparrows," Hog says, and the blend? "It's five percent whiskey!"

We're calm while we eat, even Weasel is quiet, not fidgeting, and Goose simply looks ill. Toward the end of breakfast, after a second cup of coffee and refusals of more pancakes, Hog says, "We'll take Mother's car… I put our disguises in there last night. We'll get there before they open, and Goose… Goose? With me? Well, Goose here, who's already in excellent character, he'll be sleeping out front… Bones, you'll be off a ways, obviously waiting to get in, but scared of the bum crashed at the door. No one will blame you. And don't worry"—he raises his pancake-stabbed fork at me—"I ironed your shirt and shit. Great colour. Hmm… And Weasel… charm us, tell us again how you're gonna get in there without anyone knowing."

Weasel grins. "They got a back door."

"They do," Hog says.

"There you go, man," Weasel says.

"Might not even be locked," Goose mutters, head on table.

"Well if it ain't, I'm locking it," Weasel says.

No one responds.

"For the challenge, idiots!"

Hog says he'll come in after I've had the chance to distract the owners with my Godspeak, after Goose has raised concern by possibly vomiting on a display ("Sweet," says Goose), and after Weasel has slipped in unbefuckingknownst. "I'll park the car out front, enter, *smash smash smash*," Hog says, swinging his teaspoon like a hammer, "and all four of us will grab what we can and go."

"Whoa," says Weasel, "that was three smashes. Who's the lucky third? Wait, I know!" Weasel smacks Goose on the back of the head.

"Fuck off," says Goose, head still on table.

Hog pauses. "Display cases, not noggins, arsebrain."

"No one gets hurt," says Goose in a girl's voice.

Well this was, essentially, what we'd planned, except that it was Monday, not next Saturday, and morning, not evening. And we all felt like mashed crap. And I realized that none of the 50 Scenarios actually dealt with things going as planned. In Scenario 11, for example, it turns out Mr. and Missus Carat Top have a pet alligator behind the counter, and another in the safe room, and in Scenario 15 they hurl raw meat at us, thus exposing Hog's fatal weakness, and who takes over? But did I point this out? Did I say let's go downstairs and run through this?

These are what's called "rhetorical questionings," Weasel interjects into my psyche. You see, Bones, no one is expected to answer these kinda questionings because no one knows the answer because there is no question being asked. Them butt-loving Greeks had Rhetor, pronounciated REE-tor, who was their god of pointless things, like nipples on dudes and ear hair, and Rhetor, he was always going around saying aren't my nipples pointless, but in, like Greek, so like, arnos myke niplos piplos? Fuck, man, I love the Greeks.

Mother mumbles Greek leek from the couch.

We help Hog with the dishes, Weasel drying, me stacking, Goose pointing out the odd missed thing ("There's a moldy plate on that lampshade, master"). Weasel sings about a jacuzzi and his Floozi and getting coozi... which he says is Eyetalian for something unspeakably freaky. It's not yet 8 o'clock and I'm thinking about my role, feeling that everyone is relying on the quality of my distraction, my belief in the need for others to believe, and I'm thinking that I'll do it like this, I'll talk about diamonds, about mankind's need for material things, about mankind's exploitation of others in order to get these material things, and I'll point out how these material things make us monsters, but no, no, that'll just get me kicked out, they'll dismiss me, so we need another approach, Lord help me we need another approach, by Jesus we need to pray, pray my brothers and sisters, pray to the Lord Almighty for our wretched souls, we who have come here to rob you blind, we who are not fit to rob anyone blind, we who are...

"Bones?"

... destined to fuck up everything we ever try to do...

"Bones? Could you get the clothes from the car?"

Such a normal man, this Hog. Shorter than former me by half a head, his hair in tight bronze curls, his face square and his eyes dark slits. A sensual mouth, though, and perfect teeth. Why, why you're the Antiweasel, Hog, and my oh my your name backwards spells Goh, which is just so darn close to Gosh, or Gob, or Ghost, golly I could just go into spasms on the floor right now Mr. Hog but maybe I should save it, my fervor, save it for the real deal? Slip your hand into Mother's addled dreams and pull out a rabbit and from that rabbit pull out a hat and from that hat pull out a squirting flower, we are doomed, brothers and sisters, we are damned to hell unless something magical intervenes. Ah, yes, maybe that old trickster Weasel will wave a tiny paw and time will stand still and we'll reconsider our plan, we'll walk out of The Carat Top and enrol in trade school, Goose will be a welder and Weasel a carpenter and Hog a plumber and hell, I can handle a little electricity, and we'll build houses, solid houses, not the flimsy kind that topple over when the winter wind comes off the sea...

It's a bright morning, a brisk breeze. I grab two trash bags of clothing from the backseat of Hog's mother's car, which apparently she drives from time to time, and the stench of Goose's get-up hits me. Piss, who knows what else. I turn and wretch in the driveway—last night's drinking, the heavy breakfast, the nerves, the knowing. But what did I know? I knew nothing. I went along.

Such a bad decision, Bones.

I bring the clothes inside. We pull Goose from

his kitchen chair and dress him, slap him, slip an amphetamine (mother's stash) in his coffee, funnel it down and hope he wakes in the car. Hog helps me with my hair, greases it up and slicks it back, does my tie, finds shoes, his own, that match my dress pants, leads me into the washroom and runs an electric razor over my stubble. Why not just do it all yourself, Hog?

Maybe every insecure coach needs an incompetent team.

And in this way we drive off into the sunset, except it's sunrise, and it's at our backs, and Weasel is practically on my lap in the front seat, Goose has the rear all to himself, and Hog slips a pink cassette tape into the tape deck and out comes something unmistakably Hawaiian, and I couldn't tell you if I'm crying, or laughing, because memory gets a little fudgy here, soft and sugary like a brain in a glass bottle. Past and present accuse each other of infidelity and the knives come out, bits of flesh are severed and to stick to the other and from certain angles you can't tell who's who anymore.

The streets are quiet but for a baby blue sedan blasting Don Ho. The sedan stops in a parking lot a block from The Carat Top but the passengers can't get a man out of the back seat. They swear at him, they kick him, they pinch their noses, they raise their arms in frustration. The stocky one gestures to the skinny ones and they file back into the sedan, swing by The Carat Top, drag the backseat bum from the car and leave him there, on the sidewalk, right at the door, then return to the parking lot a block away. Cameras capture it all. The bright morning shadows are long.

And what was the time frame, officer?

Uh, between 7:09 a.m., and 7:17 a.m., Your Honour.

*In Which We are Stupid*

"Fuck," says Hog as we turn a corner and see the diamond shop. We had been feeling good about things, smiling widely, music-infused, Hog whistling with the alley birds, and then "Fuck," says Hog, as we see two dogs, and Goose, see the two dogs sniffing through Goose's fragrant layers, one pulling his shirt sleeves and the other his pant legs while Goose makes only the faintest of gestures, a dreaming man swatting at a buzzing fly. "Fuck, fuck, and fuck again," hisses Hog, "that's going to draw attention. Save him. Save that goose's neck."

I run best I can in Hog's too-small leather

shoes, trying to turn my grimace to a smile of purest intention, because there are the proprietors now, he holding her back, she raising her purse, readying to swing, though at the dogs or at Goose I do not know. The dogs hesitate, check both directions of the sidewalk, the running Saviour, the Diamond Dealers, and then decide to flee across the street, but not before a leg is lifted and Goose is baptized.

I arrive out of breath, say something like oh dear Lord this poor soul, peed-on and destitute, may the Lord have mercy. Missus says, "Bums will be bums, but I can't have such an ass in front of my store," and Mister says, "I will call the authorities right away, Luv."

"No... no need!" I say, still panting. "I know this man, he's from my uh, my flock, my uh... fu—parish! Gustav! Gustav my son..."

"Well tell him to take his stink elsewhere, Father...?"

Shit, I realize I hadn't thought of a name.

Shit, I'm not supposed to be a Father.

"Father Marrow," Hog says, slapping me on the back, "beautiful morning isn't it? Always helping the poor sots of the world, aren't we? Where's the money in that? Ah, but this one's a fine mess, eh? Down on his luck and no friend of dogs, huh?"

Hog helps me drag Goose away from the doors and prop him to a sitting position. He slaps Goose a little but Goose is drooling, head lolling. "Plan b," Hog whispers. "OK," I whisper back, not knowing what plan b is, though certainly it doesn't involve Goose, and plans not involving Goose were not in the playbook. "Improv and instinct," Hog says, then stands, straightens his clothing (business attire) and enters the store. "Goose," I say, "Goose, God is asking you to wake the fuck up, God is asking you, nay commanding you, to vomit your sins on the golden display cases of the rich. Goose!"

Goose is out, Hog is in, and where's Weasel? Instinct, Hog? Instinct says get out, instinct says run, run calmly, but run and don't stop running, run into the river, grab hold of something deep in the polluted murk and don't let go. Instinct says burrow into the muck, you worm, burrow deep and leave but one eye-stalk to watch the world. An eye-stalk that darts back into the brainpod at every passing shadow.

"God be with us," I say, making the sign of the cross over my chest, making my way into the store where there's a commotion already (run away, Bones), something toward the back, in the safe room. "And what is the trouble here," I try to say loudly, like I'm fucking Moses, but what comes out is shaky, querulous, and I the safe room Weasel looks up, Weasel who's on the floor beneath Hog, Hog who's being watched over by Mister, and Mister who's saying, "The police are on their way, Father, found him stuck between the door and the doorframe, squeezing in" and Weasel saying, "Nah, man, it's the other way around, I was between the doorframe and the door and I was squeezing out," and Hog, sitting on Weasel, trying to take his coat off (Hog's, not Weasel's, because Weasel travels light, remember?), so I help him with it, and the way Hog hands me the coat tells me something, because he hands it opened wide, and so I hold it like that, briefly shielding the two of them from Mister's eyes and see Hog whisper to Weasel who starts to laugh, kicks his legs it's so funny, then starts moaning saying, "But I had to, I had to see her one more time. Bunny, Bunny, I'm sorry I lost the key, baby, oh baby" and Mister is saying, "Bunny? Bunny?" and here comes Bunny, Missus Carat Top, armament in hand, peeking over Hog's shoulder and trying to get a better look at Weasel who weasels out from under a genuinely surprised Hog and is saying, "Baby, just one more kiss, baby, just one deep, lingering" (wraps his arms around himself) "smoochie before I go, my ship is sailing today baby" and Mister is saying "Dammit, not again, Bunny!"

"Not this one," Bunny shouts, raising the handgun. "Too odd!"

Weasel looks hurt.

Sirens?

"Aw, Bunny, just one kiss?"

Bunny readies the pistol and Weasel hits the floor, crawls to the half open door while Hog goes for Mister, and I, I who was just seconds from pleading that we all calm down and pray, pray for guidance and light and deliverance from lust, which would have worked wonderfully, because my fucking tie was perfect and my shirt the colour of sunset in Heaven, well I throw Hog's coat over Bunny's scrunched-up face, lunge for the pistol and have my hands on it as it goes off once, twice, and I fall atop Bunny, who smacks her carrot top hard on the floor, who then, poor creature, has my head hit her head—oh and Mister over there is gasping because one of those hasty shots decided to visit his large intestine, poke through his stomach and liver before coming out, quite astonishingly, with not enough force to pierce his horrid lime-green vest and somehow, somehow roll down into Mister's back pocket, which he sits on before slouching over and, for Christ's sake, dying.

I, meanwhile, as Hog and Weasel slip out the back (while the police charge in through the front, ignoring Goose puking in the gutter), am quite thoroughly unconscious, lying atop Bunny in the safe room, Hog's grey sports coat the only thing between Bunny's never-to-be-kissed-again lips and mine, and a dream, of passing fish, eyes averted, soon lost in the dark river.


*My Body Lies Over the Ocean, the Sea*

I'm a bad sheep, lazy in the morning, a bad sheep who avoids the flock, avoids the sun, a bad, sad sheep. I'm a sheep who wallows in the past, who doesn't even see the bowl of oats the goat has slid in front of his face.

The night was without sleep for this bad sheep.

There was a psychologist, before the operation. He said, Do you find it humiliating, the verdict? The jury was unanimous, you know. Well, there was one abstention, but that member, Loris, she always vetoes sheep, having grown up on a sheep farm in Tasmania, fought off the devils day and night, she and Gary Checkerboard, which was the name of her faithful collie. She agreed, though, that if sheep had to be the choice, you were fine sheep material. Oh that's funny. But you haven't answered my question, and you seem to be in shock.

At one point I wandered about the barn and Fergus did not stir, but goats are not known for vigilance. The entrance to Hades was not protected by a three-headed monstrous goat. You didn't have to slip past the sleeping beard before it woke and ate all your buttons. I climbed atop a bale of hay and looked out an open window and saw the starry night, saw stars that moved over ocean, stars of aircraft, and managed to keep my sheep awe at bay.

What about my body, I'd asked, tremor in my voice. Oh yes, he said, there's a spanking new facility on our little island, Conquestador, you know the one? Those natives put up a hell of a fight! It's a fine vacation spot, you'll love it there. Well, haha, your *body* will, as long as FakeBrain doesn't decide to feed itself to the sharks again! Something about cliffs that it can't resist. Survival instincts, so tricky to create. You look concerned! Don't be. Yours, he said softly, is a life sentence, your body belongs to the State now, and rightfully so. The Constock program isn't cheap, friend. Hug yourself while you still can.

I'm innocent.

Oh yes, he chuckled. Yes! Innocent! Which brings us back to the question: do you feel humiliated by the verdict? OK, don't answer that. Of course you do. But as it's written, "Ye who are but sheep may be soft in thine eye, but thine tongues are forked like the Serpent; Thou bleatest thine Innocence yet the wolf's blood drips warm from thine muzzle."

And he laughed.

They'd sent him to examine my brain from the outside in, to look deep into my mind to make certain the psychopathic had been excised. That it had never been there in the first place merited no consideration, because it's there in everyone, I was told. There will be no more fun and maims at Moll's Farm, he said. We learn fast.

So why not slaughter the pig?

Oh now that would be immoral—this time the mistake is ours, not his. Hold still. He rapped a knuckle on my temple. Do you feel pain?

Other than humiliation, you mean?

Oh, do you associate humiliation with pain? Interesting, interesting.

Marking it down. I hadn't longed for my body, my former body, since coming to awareness of my sheepness a few days ago. I mean, the things I owned, few as they were, I thought of those as mine, my things, but was anything more mine than my body? Didn't take long for panic to set in at that thought, knowing my fingers were stroking my hair or my hands were holding my (empty!) head and I missed my toes, my thighs and good God, what did I have for a penis now? I'd never checked. I wouldn't do it. I was having a BAD spell, Body Awareness Dissociation, had been warned, had been warned by the good doctor, just between you and me, he'd said, do not think about it, not one minute, we think that's what happened to Squidley and McKraken, catatonia, all stare no meow, haha. It's supposed to be part of the punishment, but what a waste of good science...

Are you scared?

\*

I started to eat the oats, but had little appetite. Fergus kept peeking out the barn door, waiting for Jack, I assumed. Or the chickens. I need to start thinking like a man, that's the conclusion I came to last night, realizing the sheep was always tempering, was always choosing follow over lead, flee over fight. See, right now the sheep was saying be good, be quiet, eat and do what the nice ugly goat says, while the man, Bones, was saying don't trust them, why are they guarding you, a goat is not your superior, nor is a dog, and Moll is a mass murderer and will always be, following has never led sheep, or men, to any good end.

But the sheep says, When all other sheep are jumping off a cliff, they must have an excellent reason.

And the problem with fighting the sheep is this: oats are no longer sweet, they need honey and cream, or you feel like a walking end-table, or your shadow is no longer a comfort and before you know it it's panic, the wolves are running through the grass and you have been chosen, their pups will play stretch-it with your innards, you hear the paws and the panting and see the grass move now and you bolt past the one-headed goat and damn, it's too late, there's the wolf, and so you run but part of you is saying it's just Jack you fucking idiot calm the fuck down but your little legs seem to flee from each other and round and round you go, the dog and the goat in pursuit.

Eventually, said the good doctor, we all die. But eventually, I believe, *this* will be the norm: we will switch bodies, live longer. But of course only the privileged will have access to this. Have you had any headaches? Nightmares? The problem, you see, is not the body, but the brain. After 100, most are fried. He shudders. Imagine a 220-year-old man, perfect health, looks to be 30, but trauma upon trauma, neurosis upon neurosis, twelve ex-wives and a list of insults and failures stacked to the moon. The grandchildren! Oh? Well, the bad dreams are to be expected, but will end after the surgery. Probably. Honestly, I can't say.

You are a forerunner; you are a key to mankind's immortality. Heady stuff for a petty thief, huh? Oh, I know you're no murderer, everyone does, don't look so shocked. Hold still.

An all-fours runner, more like it, followed by a goat and a dog, a sheep being shepherded to an abandoned school bus while in the field the other sheep make way, part the woolly sea for what surely is the sacrificial lamb. What do they *know*? What can I *read*? No sheep has ever left the square, they say. Beware the square, they say. Bewaaaare!

The chickens pecking at the seats, the chaos. Down the stairs fumbling all legs and bulk and black-caped Moll in the shadows, waiting, and his chickens, and the knowledge, right there, right then, that what I had smelled upon leaving the square last night was not earth, or roots, was not clay nor

manure. It was carnage.
*Sleep well, little sheep?*

# Part Two

## WHEN THE LION PLAYS WITH THE LAMB

*Fergus, Or He Who Wears the Horns*

*In the hours after he escaped the square, setting free the rabbit slaves and burying Moll the Pig under an avalanche of wormy topsoil, a change came about the world. Foxes and wolves emerged from the tall grass, bowed down and covered their shamed heads, and skinny cats dropped mice from their teeth. In the dim dusk, men in abattoirs knew for the first time the sad eye of the cow, and their blades clanged to the floor. And the blackclad thief, skulking on the rooftop, threw himself into the air and was taken by the wind. The sun set with an ultra golden hue. The elimination of Utter Evil, which Moll the Pig represented in its truest form, had finally come upon the world, and the Man Who Was a Lamb, and the faithful flock who followed him, they moved like a wave across the fields. In the distance, the city glowed.*

If only it had gone that way.

Moll led me down the tunnel, while Fergus brought up the rear. We passed the rabbit feeding station and a cave of sleeping badgers and entered what appeared to be a map room of sorts, scrawls and squiggles on the wall, the floor, arrows pointing to houses and what looked like animal pens—more Constock to rescue?—and X's next to each pen. A couple of chickens, hens, were standing before the dirt-wall map, tilting heads and pecking at the X's. I wanted to stop and scratch out *escape or rescue?* but Moll moved on and Fergus nudged me and I really should have eaten more of those oats this morning, really should have at least nibbled some grass in the field, and fuck, a coffee would have been fantastic, and a bit of sausage, some bacon, pancakes and syrup and I had no idea where Hog, I mean Moll, was leading me. Hey, maybe the pig had the same desire, a little breakfast, or a big breakfast in his case, a mountain of croissants and butter, but no, no, think about those boys, Bones, think about the sickness, not breakfast, think about the lurid newscasts that made you turn away and ask Weasel how mankind ever climbed to the top the evolutionary ladder, Bones, and think about grass, and think about sun, and think about escape. And no doubt your brain is lost, claustrophobic, searching for the same old familiar panic but finding closets full of id invaders, and shutting down, denying...

But your brain comes back to you when it truly needs to, more beggar than thief, but undeniably there.

Everything is scattered here. The pockets of light, roots throwing neuronal shadows, the mice scampering and a glint of rabbit eyes, yet Moll leads on, deeper, the air cooler and soon there's no light at all, soon the soil is damp, then puddled, but you follow the farting pig because the pig knows what's ahead the pig knows all and eventually the tunnel begins to slope up, eventually light returns and you hear sounds, Bones, you hear so many sounds. You hear chickens, and sheep, you hear goats and maybe even a cow or two. The sound of dogs barking sets your fleece on end but you follow the good pig, the pig who knows where all tunnels lead, the famous mass murderer, Moll the Pig.

Guilty of 72 counts of aggravated mutilation leading to slow death.

Guilty of innumerable sexual peccadilloes with corpses.

Guilty of inspiring the Constock program and Play Prisons.

Guilty of increasing the advertising revenue in seven major news networks.

Guilty of three bad movies.

Guilty of the reformation of Wicklow Guillotine & Razor Co., out of business for 134 years.

Guilty of my sheepflesh bodysuit.

Guilty of making 9 jurors vomit for 28 days.

The room was small, dark. Moll squealed above the din of animal voices, but the voices did not stop. If anything, they got louder. Moll squealed again, and I realized his excitement was growing, that it wasn't silence he wanted. Moll squealed, squealed, and each squeal was the sound of my skin being ripped from my body. Odd that I now thought of it as *my* body. Moll abruptly left through a curtain and the cheers grew. That was from the square, I knew, and behind me, I knew (because I could smell them), just down the tunnel, there were dogs. A chicken poked its head through the curtain, light haloing its feathered head. It clucked.

The curtain, I saw, was sheepskin.

There was no secret here, nothing had been hidden from me. Behind me I saw a rabbit cowering in a corner. Farther behind me, unseen, unheard until now, was a voice that had been repeating, *Bones, wake up*, for hours. And behind that voice, there was an unending scream. The rabbit moved, scratched an ear, then went back to shivering. So, little guy, what should I do? Refuse to reach in and grab the prize? Charge down the tunnel? What awaits me? Is it Moll? Yes, it must be Moll. Moll would need his daily pound of flesh. And after, the chickens. They'll peck my bones clean.

No, chickens don't do that, says the rabbit. They are eaten, not eaters.

I guess you're right. Any advice on how I should fight the pig?

You are stupid, big sheep. It is not the pig.

Really? It's not Moll out there?

The rabbit shakes its head, ears swishing in the shadows.

Who then? What then?

Oh you will seeeee, says the rabbit.

Right then a chicken rushed in, clucking up a storm. The noise from above had been increasing. Chickens held the sheepskin curtain open and I was blinded, squinted my eyes and trotted out into the sun, the square in the ground. I had no plan of attack, nothing to plead, supposed I would run around and around until caught, maybe sink my teeth into my attacker before succumbing, one last gnash against the cruel world.

I was born poor, and I was given nothing, and I would die expecting nothing. That will be my epitaph, I told Weasel, but there was no one here to tell it to now. Shit. I had yet to look up, so I did, saw, overlooking the four edges, looking down at me, sheep, sheep, and more sheep. Excited sheep, fearful sheep. And one cow. And Jack, who barked when we made eye contact, as if to say, Hey there!

Moll, black cape flowing to the packed earth, stood before of me, and between us, flat on the ground, there was another sheepskin, bloodied at the edges. I couldn't see what stood behind Moll.

Chickens rushed in and scrolled back the sheepskin. Scrawled in the dirt:

*Little Sheep, you have been tried
and found Unworthy
of entering the Animal Kingdom!*

I thought the exclamation point a little unnecessary. And what a sham this was! Who the hell wanted to be part of the Animal Kingdom? I'd made no application and have done a lousy job of impersonating a sheep, still couldn't make a passable sheep sound. And no lawyer? Tried *in absentia*? *Again?* And who the hell can even read here? That could read *You're so pretty let's dance under the moonlight* and the crowd would still want blood.

A breeze blew in the square, raising dust. I expected Moll to charge, canvas cape flying, a slow motion movie scene, more horse than pig, and I would turn, or roll, or leap, yes, and his teeth would snap at me, perhaps just miss my soft belly, and I would come down, roll, come up firing, pistols snapping back. But Moll simply moved aside, waddled to a corner, and I saw my executioner. And although I was first distracted by what my executioner wore—some sort of crude black headgear with two filthy metal horns attached—I did quickly recognize Fergus, who last I saw had been behind me, but must've slipped away, and you're still fucking ugly.

Jack barked: Hooray Fergus! Above, sheep and cows dreamed of wearing the Horns of Justice while, inside the square, the chickens sharpened their spurs. Life is so unpredictable, I was thinking, because I had often wondered about my death, had wondered if it would be slow, like cancer, or dumb, like falling down stairs, or sudden, like lightning. And I wondered if I were allowed to watch my death in advance, would I? Weasel said he wouldn't, not a chance, while Goose said he'd do nothing but, would watch until he died of starvation, which would mean he'd be watching a video of himself watching a video of himself starving to death while watching a video... Too fucking freaky, man! Yeah, but you know what I'll be watching, Weasel? I'll be watching farm animals in a pit, I'll be watching a sheep and a really hideous goat wearing S&M headgear and there's this pig wearing a tent and where the hell am I? It's my death, the video assures it, but where am I? Weasel checks the credits. Says here you're the sheep, man.

Maybe I'm finally skydiving, chute fails to open, and that's where I land?

No man, says right here: *Death of Bones by Fergus, a Damascus Goat. Bones is indicated by the red X.* Red X, that's the sheep, man.

Maybe I land on the sheep?

Press play and let's see.

*Video has been deleted*. Huh.

Fergus charged, or maybe faked a charge, but it was enough to get me moving.


### *Holy Crap: Local Priest Charged in Fatal Robbery*

Bunny's breath was hot in my ear, the dream had

changed from fish to foul, and I was lying in a bathtub of raw meat, covered in blood, and from the raw meat a shrivelled, long-nailed hand kept stabbing out, reaching for my penis. I had to sing, had to sing away the hag hand but I had no voice.

"Grandpa's dead," I hear.

And I hear voices on radios, sirens, street names, quick feet.

I hear, "Let's get these two apart," and soon my ear cools, though it's quite wet. Bunny, I realize, likes tuna.

I'm rolled onto my back, my shirt is opened, my eyes are checked. I moan for the ache in my head, hands are going through my pockets but I've nothing in them. I sit up and am told to take it easy, then someone says, "No blood here and grandma's got a pulse." I rub my wet ear against my shoulder and wince in pain. A neck brace is attached. A gun is carried away. And me, too.

In the ambulance I hear "concussion." I hear, "Crooks smacked him from behind, looks like." And in the hospital I hear, "His name is Father Marrow, the old gal says he was a saint, an angel."

Later someone asks my name and I say Marrow but there's a hmm in response. "What church?" the man asks and I say, "I don't know, Our Lady of

Ineption, I think," then act all foggy.

During the night there's a hand on my head, another holding mine, whispers, and I wake to find a rosary. I'm surprised it hasn't burned a hole in my chest. With morning comes clarity and with clarity panic. Have they taken my fingerprints? Would they do that? No sooner had I sat up in bed then a nurse came by and asked if she could help me to the washroom, and in fact she could, and did, and while on the toilet I considered my options, which were escape and hide, stay and tell all, stay and fake amnesia, and some story about a small-time criminal named Bones looking so much like me, people even say we were separated at birth. They must be twins! The dark and the light, how amazing.

But it doesn't take long. I'm eating breakfast after being told the concussion isn't so bad, after being told that Bunny is thriving but sad and *so* angry and that maybe I could pay her a visit soon. I'm eating my last breakfast as a free man, rubbery egg whites and stale fruit, when a police officer enters, and another. I'm told I'm no Father, that I'm more of a mother—fucker, the other officer adds—and I'm told my prints match everything, from some shady character who goes by Bones, usually Bones Malone, sometimes Bones Molloy, but usually just

Bones, birthplace unknown, to the getaway sedan, the Ho-mobile, to the gun that fired the bullet that felled the old shopkeeper Harvey aka Mister Carat Top.

I'm told they have the others, too, and there was quite a battle. Three officers wounded by an old woman with a shotgun, face painted like a mad baboon, shouting nonsense. We got her though. And the others, those who were hiding in her basement. And you're in so much trouble.

It's all over the news. The nurses and doctors gather round the TV they've rolled into my room, watching the grainy black-and-white footage of us in the parking lot, us in the alleyway, Weasel slipping in the back way, getting stuck, the struggle, the pleading, the lunge by me, the blank spot in the footage, the camera shuddering back to life and my mates rushing out, Weasel returning for Hog's sports coat and then the police, the head scratching.

Looks of disgust from the nurses. "Where's the fucking rosary?"

*Well, it's clear that the sicko pretending to be a Man of the Cloth grabbed the gun and first shot the camera, then shot poor Harvey, who wasn't armed, and was old, and often gave to several local charities. Who knows how many the sicko would have killed had he not been brought down by the now-grieving widow.*

*Sicko*, they all turn and whisper.

Within a day I'm discharged from the hospital, told my brain is as fine as it needs to be, am put in jail, am given a lawyer, am soon told that I'm seriously fucked, that my gang, my buddies, have reached deals for lighter sentencing, that they're throwing me to the lions, for the lions are hungry, and bored, and things get worse from there. I don't sleep, I don't eat. I begin to feel lonely, missing the gang. My lawyer tells me my family, located this morning, legally disowned me three years ago, had all records wiped, birth certificate bought from the state and officially negated. A bonfire, a funeral of sorts. "Touching video, actually. They saw it coming, Bones. Very proactive, that family of yours."

And soon I'm raging, kicking chairs, pounding fists on knees, tables, windows. I write long letters of explanation to the media, only to have them publicly analyzed and dismissed. Judging from his use of grammar, I read, his long sentences and tendency to jump from tense to tense, not to mention his over-reliance on the comma and his latent disdain for the semicolon, we are clearly dealing with a psychopath. We even have evidence of poetic leanings and rumours of juvenilia, an unfinished science fiction romance written in his virgin years. This is worrisome, as it's an indication of excessive masturbation, which is proven to addle the mind.

*This is the route of many criminals?*

This is *the* route of all criminalia. There are variations, yes, an example of which is Sylvester Moll. He, you may remember, wrote greeting card poetry while killing seventeen boys and girls during his most active summer.

"Isn't this ridiculous?"

My lawyer lays a magazine over the newspaper I'm reading. It's glossy but smells of manure. The cover shows a series of animals, each one smaller than the other, and the headline, *What are the Limits?* In twenty years, I read, human-to-bird brain transplants may be the norm.

Easier to feed, care for, and to cage. Clip the wings and what worries do you have?

"Page forty," says my lawyer.

I flip through the journal as my lawyer leaves, barely seeing what's before me, the advertising of security systems, of robot girls who don't lie, of a car without locks, or doors, for that matter. I see the main article on page 12, advances in neural compaction, read how the ratio is currently 2 to 1, soon to be 3 to 1 (three brains in one braincase) but a ratio as high as 30 to 1 may one day be possible. The next article wonders if criminal activity is linked to a strain of rhinovirus, noting that both colds and crooks are everywhere, but then it's on to page 40, the latest Constock news, the perfection of goats and sheep, the new quota, a photo of the Prime Minister waving a finger, and the watch list.

Which I'm not on.

Because it's too soon, of course. It's too soon.

My kind lawyer, however, has a yellow highlighter and loves to use it.

The standards have been overly high, says an unnamed government official. Which of course made sense, he continues, as we had to ease the program in, allow the population to get used to the idea that this is the future of punishment, of justice. We didn't expect such overwhelming approval. One could say it borders on delight, yes? So we're going whole hog with it, forgive my pun, and soon legislation will be introduced. The article goes on to state that any offense previously subject to a 10-year sentence will now be eligible for Constock. The government is buying up unprofitable farms and retrofitting them. Graphs show that within a few years the Constock program will be significantly less costly than the outdated, rather medieval penitentiary system. Red barns instead of grey prison cells. Pastoral, idyllic, fair.

A kind of Utopia, for us on the outside

Personally, says the government official, I think any criminal should face these consequences. It's a known fact that petty crime begets serious crime, so we have to treat the petty pretty seriously.

My lawyer returns, hands me a coffee, and I ask him what my chances of this are. He shrugs, says, "Fifty-fifty?" Says, "Nah, higher." Says, "Yeah higher." Winces, doesn't look me in the eye.

"What do you know?"

"Yeah, about that."

"I haven't even had a trial yet."

My lawyer wobbles his head.

"What does that mean?"

More wobbling.

"There is, like, a shine in your eyes!"

My lawyer covers his mouth, stomps on his foot, sets his face to stolidity, says, "I will do everything I can to make sure you are a free man, but you should prepare for the worst. Actually you should probably accept it. Yeah, that's better."

"When do I go to trial?"

"When do you want to?"

"What? I can choose?"

"No. Of course not. Did you read the condom ad on page... he leafs through the journal... ah, this one!"

"I don't care about the fucking *ad*..."

"Read it!"

The Prime Minister, in hunter's regalia...

"We will win this case, Bones."

At his feet, three women in dog masks, naked if not for the leopard print bikinis...

"You're sure about it?"

Shoulder shrug.

"Can I fire you?"

The PM's rifle, held at crotch level: WHAT WOULD HE DO?

"Can't fire me."

I sleep that night on a narrow cot, bitten by bedbugs and dreaming of something at the door, some beast, and Weasel calling down the hall, and I know I can get out of my cell if I angle my body so, but I keep getting stuck and the beast is near, breathing on my neck, salivating. I sleep fitfully, wake screaming and am returned to the hospital. In the morning I have a visitor.

## Rope-a-Goat

"You know, Bones," said Hog one night in Ye Olde Bear, "they called him Sillywilly Molly in school, and it made him angry. Now what if the little prickholes hadn't called him that? Think about it. There's a boy out there, or there used to be a boy out there, because he's a man now, likely in a management position, a bully who started it all. Some cross-eyed wanker without a clue what a dick is for, and he changes the world. Blows my mind, Bones."

Hog points a stubby finger to the television, unheard over the bar chatter. "Oh, this part is ironic, Bones." This is the day after the surgery, the day Moll was Swine, and it's Hog's play by play that I remember, in the pit, the square, with horned Fergus charging. "Here, Bones, listen, he's saying that man is a predator, it's fucking great. That man is an animal beneath it all, and sometimes there's a spark that rises up, just fucking hear his thick accent. That there's this spark that rises and catches fire on the dry embers of civility, it's just waiting there, and some of us are drier than others. Fucking great, fucking brilliant, Bones."

At the word 'brilliant' I shift to the right and Fergus charges past, but quickly takes to the charge again and if not for an abrupt stop, drop, and roll, I would have been fully gored. The goat is quicker than you'd expect. Comes again and I'm not a healthy sheep, you know, maybe it's asthma, or the previous owner had a three-pack-a-day habit. Comes again and I run toward the bystanders, the chickens, who cluck and scatter and fly at eye level, feathers everywhere and oh dear, one's impaled itself. Blood runs down the horn but Fergus, the old pro, shakes it off.

The crowd goes wild. Howls and clucking and a crashing accordion of goat laughter.

The sheep watch silently.

I try darting to the left, to the right, to the left, to the right, wanting to loosen the headgear as Fergus follows my movement. And maybe it'll blind him a little, close off his peripheral vision and I'll kick him in the ribcage. I see Moll in the corner, in the cool shadows, lying down, staring, drooling. I see the sheep above, heads jerking side to side. I see Fergus charging, the headgear a little looser (and who the hell or what the hell made that gear?) but my shifting has left me dizzy. Perhaps my brain is a little loose in its cage, perhaps it's been sloshing about all this time, bruised, drunk on fermenting brain cells, or perhaps I'm just a sheep in a field, wide-eyed and wobbly and having visions. Sure no one pays attention to the sheep that sees, the sheep that bleats the apocalypse. He's addled, they say, so keep your distance.

And maybe I *am* Chosen, because there's no way I should get out of this. The goat has experience and no moral conscience. The goat was made to charge, to butt, and little sheep were made to run straight to the slaughterhouse. A sheep should leap upon the horns, find the searing pain tragic but delicious, knowing that to fight is to delay the inevitable, that the only happy place is the place where sleep rains falling sheep, heaven is a moonless night, and no wolf tracks your shadow. And like the rabbit that goes limp when rolled onto its back, offer your belly, your innocence, to the cruelty of the world, hoping it softens it just a little.

I offer Fergus my belly.

Well, actually, I topple, fall forward and in a panic, freeze. Momentum rolls me onto my back and my horned executioner must be startled, because though he lowers the horns and goes for the kill, he misses, badly, and I'm below the goat, belly to belly, could snap the ugly fuck's scrotum with my teeth, but there's no need, for the goat is stuck, horns in the earth. I scramble out.

The crowd, stunned.

In a burst of exuberance my back legs kick out and fly into Fergus's raised flank, knocking the goat to the ground and freeing him from the stuck horns. *Shit*, I think, *don't get cocky, Bones*. I turn, preparing for the charging head, preparing for more evasion, a death that'll be more bludgeon than gore, but Fergus is going the other way, Fergus is looking for a hole to hide in, exposed for the goat he is. Oh I know you now, Fergus, you lackey—take the mask away and what do we have but a wannabe. Follow the Pig, you were told, and you too will have the pale crescent badge, the gift of soil scribble, and maybe even your own cape.

And then, of course, the squeal.

So a sheep walks into a bar, orders an ale and says, "Hey mates, so like there I was, in this underground version of a Roman arena—underground, but you know, open to the sky? Imagine sheep and other farm animals watching from above. And I had to fight to the death! At first it was a goat, but the goat was like, wearing headgear, with sharp spiky horns. What do you mean, goats already have horns? This one didn't, and no goat has horns like that. Anyway." Yeah so the sheep walks into a bar and orders an ale but no one's paying attention anymore, the

TV flickers high, men chase a ball, men run from bulls, men grapple each other on a mat, hunt each other with paint, knock sticks against balls, race over hurdles, around bases, through end zones and there's channel after channel after channel, too many to flip through to see that black market video, the one showing on the channel whose number no one remembers for long, it has a string of zeros, that's all, no one but a few late-night drugged-up fans who live for this shit, get off watching the goat take on all comers (mostly dimwitted sheep, but also clumsy cows and the saddest of pigs), the goat that's never lost a bout, the horns that once shone but are now blood rusted. Rumours are this is Constock, animals with, like, people brains, fighting it out, rumours are Sylvester Moll is behind all this and no one does anything, the Prime Minister himself is a huge fan, and rumours are that this tape is different, that this wasn't supposed to get out, that the pig is raging over it and vowing vengeance. Maybe in the bar an unseen TV is flickering, changing of its own ghostly will, maybe three recently-freed ex-cons have their backs to it and don't the see the goat topple and retreat, don't see the caped pig rise from its corner and charge at the hero sheep who turns at the sound of the squeal, turns and against all common sense charges toward the charging pig and appears to fly upon contact, fly so high that yes, he flies clear of The Pit and lands tumbling but running atop his soft brethren and keeps running, heading for the green hills, the setting sun, his only pursuer an elated border collie.

"So what was ya sayin'?" The man at the bar turns to his new companion, but the talking sheep is gone.

## *Robyn, Bedrest*

"PETABBY", says the dark-haired nurse whose breath smells like mint. "We will help you," she whispers through full, glossy lips, the p sticking, releasing to an adorable, tiny o. She slips her hand beneath the crisp psyche-ward sheet and I find myself wondering what those angels are called, the full-service ones that so many radical fanaticals blow themselves to bits for.

Her hand stops on my belly, resting just above the bellybutton, and my breathing quickens. "Oh dear," she says, moving her hand in circular motions, "Oh dear you're so frightened, just like a little bird. Oh no no don't be afraid. We will help you." Her eyes, her dark eyes water and she sucks in her luscious lips and her brow furrows and whether she's oblivious to my erection or simply sees it as a perfectly permissible act of fear, I do not know, and do not care.

"They're going to take you away today," she says, "but we won't let them. Well, OK, we can't really do anything today, but..."

Commotion. The nurse drops down and hides as the door opens and a police guard looks in, looks the room over but does not enter. His eyes dart toward the ceiling and he mutters sorry and shuts the door. Saved by arousal. Some men don't respond well to another man's erection.

There's something on my stomach. A business card. Her name, Robyn, a phone number, and PETABBY above it. Password to heaven? Image of a children hugging farm animals. "We can't do anything today," she whispers, still crouched on the floor, showing a red bra and cleavage that makes me weep. Carry me away, please? "We have someone on the inside," she says, "and it isn't good." She looks up, makes her lovely-sad face again. "It's horrible what they're doing. Those poor... "

She shakes her head, stands slowly, sets a hand on my thigh.

"Heeey, you're not really a nurse." My first words.

"Shh," she says.

"I'm Bones," I say.

"Shhhh," she says.

"I love the way your lips move when you shush me, they way your chin juts forward and the soft pale skin on your neck seems to offer itself to my mouth."

She pats my thigh. "They have you on drugs, Bones, to keep you calm." Calm my ass, I think, seeing my erection bunching the sheet inches from her hand. "You should be screaming," she continues, "you should be jumping out the window, but instead you're lying back, muttering sweet nothings. I am so angry!"

Again the door opens and we work in unison this time, she rolling me to my side, saying, "Now just relax and let go," and feeling an ice cold bedpan slide against my penis. "The fucking drugs," she says, "he can't take a goddamn piss without assistance." I can't see who opened the door, but from the voice it must be another nurse, one who says, before leaving, "Don't do him any favours, sister."

"See," she says, "they drug you, keep you calm, keep you aroused so you can't think. I'll have to think for you, OK?"

"I really do need to pee."

"You shouldn't do anything, not right away."

"OK. But..."

Hovering over the bedpan, my erection starts to shrivel.

"We haven't really planned this out. PETABBY is still so new. I mean, just last week we were PASCAL, then I'm told we're PETABBY here are the new cards. It's cuter, yes, and it was my idea, though Wren, our leader, is taking credit for it. But if we keep changing names, how will anyone take us seriously?"

She puts her hand on my forehead, then runs her long, red-nailed fingers through my hair, sighs, her eyes tearful. "Poor things," she says. "This is where they'll cut you," fingernail arching across my skull.

At that, my erection dies.

She takes the business card back, says, "You can't use this here. We'll hide one at your place, under that broken flagstone you always trip over, OK?"

"What if someone fixes it?"

"We'll break it again!"

I roll onto my back and she sits at the side of the bed. She seems a bit scatterbrained, to be honest, a touch unsure, but her nurse's outfit isn't regulation, shows too much leg, too much cleavage, and someone has to tell her. Wouldn't want her to get caught, found out, marched into a back room by the other nurses, forced to strip naked, tied up, lashed even. "Those legs," I say, for apparently I am drugged, "could heal many a sick man, Robyn." "Shhh," she says, "don't use my name, dummy."

I go silent. She plays with the hem of her skirt. "All those poor little innocents," she says. "We had to do something, we couldn't just... just..."

I reach out, pull her next to me, we lay side by side. Her hair smells like honeydew melon. "They tell me not to get involved," she says, "they tell me 'your heart is too big, Robyn.' They tell me I should not be an operative for PETABBY, but I tell them answering phones never saved anyone. Then Wren says '911, duh, suicide hotline, hello?' Oh, no one understands me." She rolls over, lays her head on my chest, holds me close. "But how can I not get involved, Bones? That's like telling a shepherdess not to protect her flock. Are you still frightened?"

"Terribly."

"I would be too, if they were going to cut my brain out."

Eyes looking into mine, fingers tugging at my

hair.

This is the story of a very confused penis.

"Robyn, what if you aren't able to rescue me, what if...?"

"We fail?"

"Yes."

She sighs. "All we do is fail. Wren says it's the trying that's important, not succeeding. We're not Navy Seals, just people who care."

"Wren's a coward."

"I'll save you, I will!"

"You don't even know me."

"What does that matter?"

"What if I'm really a killer?"

"But the donkey isn't, dummy."

"Huh?"

She sits up, seems to float above me, then settles atop. "OK, first, I know you're not a killer. We've got someone on the inside, remember? And second, do you even know what PETABBY stands for? Don't you read the news? What have you been doing the past week?"

She leans forward, so close that I can feel the heat cradled between her breasts. Universes are born there. She pulls back the sheet and scratches the letters on my chest. "P is for People. E is for Ethical.

T is for Treatment. A is for animals', with a plural possessive. And B is for bodies."

"And the B and Y?" I gasp.

"Tabby! Like the cat! It's just, it's nice. It's cute."

"Beats PETAB, I guess."

"See? You get me."

"Robyn…"

"Shhh!" She puts a finger to my lips, listens. The footsteps in the hallway move on. She sighs, rolls the sheet back up, says, "I think someone's getting too involved again."

"Who? Not me."

Leaning forward, she kisses my forehead, a kiss of death, a kiss for St. Lazarus, patron saint of lost erections, kisses my forehead and is no longer on the bed, is no longer in the room, is no longer anywhere near the sad little voice in my head, the one that had been waiting to say this may be my last chance to know passion, to know the only real reason for our existence, Robyn.

"Cut my fucking brain out," I mutter while rolling over and trying not to cry as my erection once again wilts like a weed in the summer heat, cut my fucking brain out as I piss into the bedpan. Cut my fucking brain out and put it in the desert, in a cactus.

*Caddlebrained*

There was a moment of silence with the psychologist, I remembered, a moment right after we'd gone through the levels of acceptance—shock, terror, denial, sorrow, and back to terror—where he said, He's not entirely crazy, you know. He stroked his white and grey beard while looking out the window, where the sun was setting and crows in the yard below swooped down on a prowling cat. He was talking about the Prime Minister, saying, He's more than just a gag reel for change, he's... like Blake. Mad, but visionary. A man before his time.

And I'd said, He seems *of* his time to me. How else does he get elected?

He said nothing, smiled, stood and rested his hand on my shoulder for a moment. He left me with documents, my rights as Constock, and a small volume of medical fact and fiction, full of illustrations. My rights were few. The right to be fed and housed appropriately in correlation to my Jailbody's needs. The right to receive no further transplants unless brain-body conflict arises. The right to receive a minimal pension which will pay for a yearly medical check-up, as well as a funeral, a burial plot, and a headstone which will bear an asterisk. Lastly, there was the right to be returned to my former body should it be proved three times without a doubt that I am innocent. Noted beneath this final right, in tiny lettering, was the fact that this technology was not currently available.

The booklet, called *From Criminal to Animal: Everything You Don't Really Need to Know, You Lousy Crook,* contained 56 pages of Constock animal fact and fiction, notes on how the human brain interacts within the Jailbody and several pages of technical data, medical jargon, and pharmaceutical arcana. At the time I had only just found out that I was (to be) sheep over sloth, and though I'd thought both would be fitting—having been called lazy more than a few times in my life—there was a thrill, wrong as that word is, that I'd be the first sloth. Slowness had its appeal. Trees all day. All of this just to say, as Jack and I raced across the field toward the setting sun, the city of long shadows, that I recalled reading about certain imbalances, such as overriding fear from prey animals (preferred in Constock), or persistent sexual response from humans (for the human animal does not come into heat, but rather remains highly charged, always seeking the pleasure of orgasm, till the age of 84), and I recalled a fascinating passage on adrenaline overproduction, especially in man-sheep Jailbodies, where a high is produced and with it a feeling of invincibility that had gotten many a man-sheep in a world of woolly trouble.

Did that happen in the square?

I felt supercharged. I felt I was more electric lash than herd animal. I was a bolt of white fire searing across the green field, and they saw my flaming spear from the city's spires. Jack, you gotta keep up, you and I, we will work wonders. No one is prepared for what will happen, Jack, no one has expected it and no one has imagined it. No single passage in all the world's scripture has predicted invasion by man-sheep and border collie. Not even vaunted Nostradamus saw this one coming, Jack. Jack? Ah, Jack had fallen back, was sitting on the crest of a small hill, his dog shoulders slumped and his shining eyes reflecting the city which burned so bright before me.

Thus the prophecies are true, my friend.

Such was my state of mind in the hours following my escape from the square, and though I felt like I had an army behind me, I didn't have Jack, as they say, as he turned without even barking, turned and vanished behind the hills, turned back to the farm life he knew where that night he'd lay sighing in the barn, thoughtful eyes staring through the hayloft opening, counting stars, not sleeping. While my legs trotted along, part of my brain dreamed and another part of it screamed, analyzed, tried to dig the foundation out from under the dreamer, was like a rush of deep, turbulent water coming upon the sea's calm surface, upon the tan man in his plastic duck, the kind that's *absolutely not a flotation device*, the tan man drinking his fruity cocktail through a straw, his neck burning to a lobster crisp around his tropical shirt's stiff collar. He has fallen asleep and is hundreds of miles from shore!

You are an experiment.

A fucking experiment.

You are fucked you fucking experiment.

Isn't Jack such a nice dog?

The city glows with an angry hue.

You are experiencing being a fucking experiment.

Are those sheep? Are sheep coming down from the office spires, are sheep spilling into the city streets and rushing toward me? Are they now bounding through the night's dew-wet meadows? Are they…?

And then my face was on fire.

*It's pretty stable*, I recalled the kind, tall shrink saying in his flute-like voice, his voice that whistled through the gate-like gap in his teeth, *it is surprisingly stable. But it's not perfect, and it can't be. Terror, that's what returns. Terror of confinement, terror of invasion, terror of being snatched up and eaten. Can't dismiss that, huh? It's unethical, but it's important. And I think importance trumps ethics. Oh, and then we can play ethics against ethics, theft against theft. For that's what they've done, right? Stolen your life, stolen your mind. Not that it's been stolen from you. Philosophically, this is fascinating stuff, Bones.*

*What, in fact, has been stolen?*

Control, I was thinking, lying on my side in the field, my delicate sheep's nose singed, stripped of a layer or two of skin. Do sheep cry? Do sheep bleat in agony? Would anyone eat anything that cried for its life moments before the killing? I suspected not, but I wasn't sheep, not fully, and though the noise I was making may have sounded inhuman, it was anything but.

Everything crashed then. My body, driven beyond its limits, began to convulse. The back of my neck throbbed and my brain ached. Blood rushed from my nose in torrents and my bowels spewed whatever remnants of my morning meal remained. I gasped for air, gasped like a lifted fish, and then drifted above the field and came back down, lay beside the tiny sheep and held it close.

No, it's not stable, said the shrink as he held his cigar. *And I don't think it will ever be.* He blew smoke out the window. *You can graft an ear onto a potato, you know, but you can't predict what it will hear.*


*Mutton for Punishment*

Wolves panting.

Weasel and Hog, in a dance-off.

Robyn, hair plastered to her forehead, rolling me to the elevator.

A ewe sidling up, those eyes saying, Ride me, stranger.

Fergus looming, fuck-ugly head blocking the sun.

Goose, first met behind a bar, pipe raised, then laughing.

Sylvester Moll Pig Doll, order now.

Barmaid Ginger that's what they called her though really Janice, yeah, took me home, tore her room apart looking for condoms.

A wolf is a bottomless pit, and you do not stare.

When there's an ache in your head and you'd rather be dead.

The sun is freaking ball of gas, Bones!

Hog's mother staring at me across the table, smiling, toes caressing my shin.

Teeth sink in.

You see it in the sun now, the incandescent shimmer, a spark and zap as a yellow butterfly goes up in smoke.

Hog saying, Bones, Bones, Bones. What do we do with you?

Through dry eyes the sun bounces, jerks like Weasel in the dance-off but the grass isn't pavement and that's your head bouncing, really. Pulled by the wolves, creamy teeth around your skinny black legs.

Face's a bloody mess, eh?

Goose setting the pipe down, still laughing.

The perimeter is patrolled by wolves, Little Sheep!

Prison riot guard brains, oh yeah.

And you're dragged along, out of your own filth, belly to the sky: they're wolves, they're people, they're guards, they're pissed.

But four legs fly, they say. Better than rolling.

Forcefield technology is a figment of my opponent's imagination, says the Prime Minister, and if he persists on insisting I will have to challenge him with my Lightsaber. Makes duelling movements, zoom-zooming sounds.

Janice Ginger you were my last summer simmer.

The field dips into a ditch and the wolves gather at a low door, nudge a panel of buttons and a gate opens. They drag you in and here we go, underground again. Mutton for supper, mutton for supper!

Don't eat the brain!

Ah, fuck Bones, let's go sit by the river and watch some legs float by.

Wolves over you, shaking heads. More wolves come, more head shaking then two barks, one bark, two barks and a mangy one appears, head low, sees you and tries to turn away but there's a bark and your face is being licked. The mangy one gags, but keeps licking.

In the washroom, wiping blood from Goose's face.

Broke my gorgeous nose.

You see the scene, bootcamp-like, a tall man in uniform and aviator glasses. Wolves in a semicircle. Too much sun. Do what you will with escapees, hurt them, play with them, hurt them. Torture is fun, am I right? am I right? am I right? Eager whining, quick sharp barks. Good guard doggies! Sheepshaped treats are thrown, snatched out of mid air, devoured.

Bones.

The mangy one slinks away and curls into a corner. No one knows that he likes the taste of blood, and not just sheep's blood. Oh no, look at those eyes, how they move slowly over the room, the black leather pet beds, the rawhide biting bars, the flatscreen panels flashing porn, both human and canine, sometimes both. The eyes stop on you, filthy sheep, scab-nosed, brain-fried Constock, they pause and change their expression. Now that's interesting, that perks your ears a little.

You pull your legs under you, sit a little more upright, watch the wolves as they scan through files on a flatscreen, paws clicking a floor-button, scanning black sheep-face after sheep-face. Look, there's no collar, so we can eat it. We have to be *sure*, Kenneth, or command will have our tails. Well then, have a blast, because I can't tell one sheep from the other. It's hot and I'm going to sleep. And send command a text, tell them to get the goddamn AC working. Sleep then, but I tell you, Greg, I've got an eye for this shit.

Scanning, scanning.

In the dance-off, Hog spins, moves with the beat, arms go up, down, knees pop in, pop out, feet slide and his shoes are always the finest. There's power in everything he does, that shaking fist, tense with rhythm, could shoot through a wall. The police watch from a distance. It's a hot night and both dancers are dripping with sweat. The crowd gathers, bets are placed, the cops tap their flatfeet to the rhythm, slap their batons into their palms. That's a great sound system in D-Dog's car, man. Subwoofer rapture. And Weasel, he's there, he's not there, body jerks like his joints travel, from head to toe and from toe to head, spasm fashion, but it's something to behold. They move closer to each other, Hog singing along, Weasel white eyed at the streetlights...

The police rush in, guns drawn. Hog and Weasel freeze.

A buzzer sounds and all the wolves look to the door.

Is it Moll?

The door opens: a wolf, a dead raccoon.

Raccoon? Too clever, too dexterous, too devious. Early experiments ended in disaster for the doctors. A scalpel was involved. Doctor brains were crudely switched. So much blood.

The police laugh, shoot up the night sky.

Back to the scanning, scanning, and there you are, wow, druggy confused eyes, number 3902, Bones formerly Bluebell-7, and for the first time in your short life as a fake sheep, almost unbidden, you make a passable sheep sound.

*The Trial of Bones Malone, Part One*

At three in the morning I'm woken and told it's time, the new courtroom is ready and the bugs must be worked out before tomorrow's important trial. I'm told to dress and take a shit or something, am handed a cup of coffee, some kind of energy wafer, and am left alone for five minutes. A prisoner jumpsuit, all off-white with a red question mark on the back. Comfortable, fleece lined, maybe a bit warm, hmm. Smells like the previous prisoner's fear. The coffee is cold, weak, and already half gone when handed to me, and the energy wafer crumbles when opened, as if it's been in a back pocket and sat upon.

I lie down on the cot and fall into a quick, jerky sleep that lasts the duration of a colour, orange, I think, with two brown sticks framing it and the word tassel is *important* and then the guard returns, pulls me to my feet, says, "Your lawyer is protesting the time of trial and won't be able to join you until at least seven, maybe eight. The trial will last till nine." This morning? What?

Was running through the forest, pursued by a fursnake, then more fursnakes, which were ropes, which coiled around my feet and would flip me, if I let them, so I couldn't let them. I had to windmill my arms and make a high-pitched, unwavering screee. And before that, a waterfall, bathing in it, but ice all around and *shit, this the exhibit, the penguins and why did I bathe here, nude, rubbing it and the audience, shaking heads, laughing.* "I don't have shoes," I say to the bearded guard, who stops, slams me against the corridor wall. "Shoes make prisoners comfy, don't they," he says with wide eyes and gritted teeth. "Shoes makes prisoners run," he says, a little singsong this time. "No shoes for you," he says, then lets me go, says, "Run, try it."

"You took my shoes, didn't you?"

He smiles.

The farther we go the narrower the corridor becomes, and eventually we have to squeeze sideways. The guard is fat, gets stuck, asks me to push him, give his hip a kick or something. I push him a little, just enough to tighten things, and now he's moving his head, oh no, he's saying, or not saying, because he's got no breath, turns blue, struggles, farts mightily, passes out. I return to my cot. Fall asleep quickly and wake in a sweat, the fleece soaked, and the guard is saying, "Sorry about that, your lawyer needed some time to get here," and there's my lawyer, saying, "Shit, dude, it's speed trial, everyone's waiting."

"What time is it?"

"It's like five..."

"Four thirty-eight," says the guard.

Running shoes are at the foot of the bed. I try to lie down again but my lawyer flicks my nose and says, "We have to find a defense, Bones, at least for show." I sit up, put on my shoes. "Um, how about I was framed? How about I never fired a shot?" "No," says my unshaven attorney, whose breath is stale-coffee foul. "No, that's really fucking boring. Make the jury laugh, Bones, none of that lame logic crap. Logic is so twenty years ago. Where have you been?"

"Who me?"

"Who else?"

"I was sleeping."

The Question Jumper sticks to me, can feel sweat dripping down my back into the crack of my butt. Never knew this before. Did you see the dude sweat? Guilty, huh? Body never lies. Let's throw the stones now. My lawyer says, "Fucking speed trial; I need a new job. A defense, Bones, a defense. Think!"

Down a stairwell, corrugated metal, dimly lit,

then a garage. Two guards ahead, two guards behind. I'm not shackled but the Question Jumper is made of Constriction Cloth and a simple press of a button by a guard and I'd be shrink-wrapped.

"Do we have my psychologist's report?" I ask.

"Why, you mental?"

"Something about not fitting the profile, maybe?"

"Anybody can kill, Bones."

"I know it, but I mean sheep, Constock?"

"I glanced through it, Bones, and it said you'd make a perfect—watch your head—and even very cute lamb."

In the back of the patrol car my lawyer says, "I really need some fucking shuteye. Night terrors, man, can't sleep a wink. Think of a defense, Bones, else your ass is in the grass." He smiles, closes his eyes, raises a finger to his mouth when I start to speak. The car speeds into the dark morning, country gangsta rap on the radio, the speed increasing with each empty thought I have. What do they have? Video of me on the scene, wrestling with Bunny. Shit. Testimony by former teachers, landlords and lovers. My gang's apparent plea bargain. My history. But murder? A defense? How about reverse psychology? I wake my lawyer, tell him this. "Sounds good," he mumbles.

All my life, ladies and gentlemen of judgement, I have wanted to be a sheep. Thank you so much for making my dreams come true.

Rustling their papers, throwing them in the air, sheepy blueprints drift down.

Make him worm!

Make him lizard!

"So the punishment would be to set you free, strike you from the Constock list," says the driver.

"What do you think?"

"It'd have to be hidden, they'd have to discover it, feel good about their brilliance. You know?"

"An yhat's zha gricky yarht, Gones," yawns my lawyer.

The car enters a tunnel, advertisements scroll along the tunnel walls. Vacation resorts, perfect teeth, cars that know your name, ask how your day was. A scent that will make your woman obey you, *Ordeur, oui oui.*

Panic.

"Are we being followed?" says the driver.

A van, tinted windows.

"Not that it matters," says my lawyer, who opens his briefcase and takes out a toothbrush, continues to talk while brushing, something about a "gillent glan, glut glairz gno gime googuhgellapgit. Agh phugket, phugkettawl."

He rolls down the window, spits.

What if I don't say anything? What if I stop being, stop wanting? What if I stop believing? My inner psychologist tells me it ain't gonna happen, dude, you're like, up against a whole lot of shaggy evolution, and things that don't want, don't pass on their genes. "You really smell," says my lawyer, who leans toward me. "Look out the widow," he says.

I look.

Car stops.

Whoa.

Suddenly I'm wearing a sheep suit, should have known it all along. How did that get past me? The guard pulls up my suit's hood, its black face and long floppy ears, pouts and says, "What a cutie this one is," and another guard says, "Careful now, gets lonely out here." My lawyer is dressed like a bunny, says his hopping isn't convincing and his goddamn bladder is full. "Have you thought of a defense yet?" His eyes are too wide, no one will believe him, but it doesn't matter as the guards turn away, put hands over mouths and fake coughing fits while my lawyer is attacked by two men dressed like foxes. He screams like a schoolgirl, kicks and claws, but a straight right from Fox Two and he's falling, body limp, backwards down the court steps, all ears and oversized feet, a brown ball rolling, and is dragged away, replaced by another bunny, and I'm wondering is this PETABBY? But the guards? No.

I look to my new lawyer, say, "It's not like we had fucking defense anyway."

Bunny lawyer hisses

The courtroom shines, has that new car smell, is black leather and brass and amber lighting that flashes to sun-bright when I enter, and there is murmur, applause, trumpets, confetti rains down and, *look*, it's my mates running out and throwing hugs around me, dancing with my furry lawyer and the guards are taking bows, the camera crews finally show themselves—ah, man, I knew I saw a looming microphone boom last week—and then a giant hand, slapping me, fuck that hurts, the sting brings tears and someone's saying "He has to go in now, maybe some salts?" A shout. "Anyone got salts? Some fucking salts?"

My lawyer says, "They have to find a better way."

A wheelchair. Sit.

Ramp.

"I think I'm going to puke," I say.

"Hit your head, sorry man."

"Wha?"

"Speed Trial rules, you know? It's too much, too soon, the accused tend to freak out, but—excuse me? Can you help me lift? But... we can't use a sedative, so... a psychotic... where's the judge?" My lawyer leaves me in the wheelchair, wanders off looking for the judge. A bailiff helps me to the Trial Seat, centre of it all, spins me once and says, "It's got great back support, Bones, really great support. Wish I had one at home. We'll help you, OK? Forget about the trial, we'll help you, *shhhh*."

The courtroom begins to fill. It's circular, deep like a concert bowl. The judge will hang from a harness above me, the prosecution and the defense team (ha!) will seemingly fly about the room. Speed Trial, yes. "Make them laugh, Bones. Are you alert now? Still need to barf?"

He hands me a paper bag, slaps me once more, checks my eyes.

"Essence of *psilocybin*," he says. "Gave you a quick injection, in the car. Sorry, bud."

Yes, the courtroom fills to the gills and there's a buzz now, my heart is pounding and there's a cheer as the prosecution enters, followed by their witnesses, the rubbery faces of Harvey the Fallen Shopkeeper, a too tall Weasel, a short Goose, and a skinny, snickering Hog.

Silence! cries the judge, six feet above my head.

*For Those Who Hunt the Men-Sheep Down*

It was during an afternoon nap in the wolves' lair that I first considered the effect not speaking was having on me, how it seemed to have heightened my skills of observation and how little love I'd ever had for conversation. Well, I'd always been a watcher, a listener, someone who spoke only when spoken to. Not that I couldn't carry a conversation, but some people just never shut up, seem to fear silence. Silence creates a void that their thoughts fill too quickly.

Weasel, the classic case. And on the other end, Goose. If Weasel's mind was a buzzing hive, Goose's was a snake, slow, but not so slow that it couldn't slide up and wrap around your throat and put an end to any quick escapes you'd counted on, you smug rodent. The wolves, I could see, fought boredom. All guards, I concluded, fight boredom. Ergo, I thought, quite satisfied with myself, they hope for an escape attempt, and will in fact aid the captive in escaping. The captive is a sheep, and the captive poses no threat. The captive is sheep and nothing but sheep. Let's chase it. And then eat it. Why had no wolf checked for my scar? Surely they knew about the surgical scar.

Longer fleece hiding it?

Admittedly, the scar could simply look like a fold of skin, or the surgeon could have enough skill to hide it. Maybe they'd managed to slip brains in through the eye sockets—I'd read that, in the *Constock News*. How long had I been sheep, then? Years? Foldable brain. Ship in a bottle. God. I'd seen no scar on Fergus, or Jack, but still.

But back to the observing, the not talking.

Or maybe they didn't want to know, didn't want to see that flesh infection, didn't want to shatter the doggy fantasy of meadow-pure sheep, succulent, ambrosia-like, where eating man-sheep would be tantamount to cannibalism. The mangy one, who needed a name instead of Two Bark One Bark Two Bark, though Two Bark would do until something better came up, and it just now occurred to me—what an afternoon of revelation—that these dogs, well wolves, these former prison guards, did not write to one another, did not try to pronounce words in that woeful way people would mistake for love, everything softened to vocal wattle, a wobbly rueful whimper and howl of an attempt. No, they barked, short barks, quick barks, soft barks, a bark that I swore was laughter, another that sounded like Goose's snicker, and mangy one's/Two Bark's almost inaudible gruff. Could I do that? Would anyone hear?

But no, I didn't know the code, the grammar. What was I thinking?

I sighed, my leg chained to a metal post at the back the canine command centre, Two Bark across the way, sighing as well. I sighed, he sighed, and the wolves at the computer terminal skipped on by the dopey-eyed mugshot of Bluebell-7, not even glancing back to do a comparison, the light in the room dimmed and a soft chime sounded, there were sighs all around as the terminals shut down and all the wolves stretched, yawned, headed for their respective leather pet beds, closed their eyes and I pretended to do the same but in fact kept observing, so much more man than sheep at the moment, envious of the wolves, their power and speed and thinking they should be smarter, shouldn't they?

But no, these were former guards, the ones not wise enough to slip out when the prison riots started, the ones too duty-bound (thus rule-bound) to run when the odds said you're dead, Fred, and the ones too stupid to see the joke in giving a life protecting society from a menace society created. We fill a niche, Hog would say, and society abhors an empty niche. We're like that sinful layer on top of the crème brulée. We're... fuck, what am I trying to say, Weasel? Weasel points to Hog. We're the fucking fantasy, the fucking superheroes. Even the creeps like Moll. Nah, especially the creeps like Moll. Anyway, that's our niche, like the spider in the crawlspace, life can't roll along if you don't smooth out the nooks and crannies with crooks and... nannies.

"Jesus it stinks down here!"

Footsteps.

"Are they sleeping?"

Close eyes, Bonesheep, close eyes.

"All asleep, sir."

"Do it quick, then. Fuck, something's rotting down here." I opened an eye just enough to see three men in dark attire, two at work on the terminal while a third checked the sleeping wolves, checked ears, teeth, spent a lot of time with Two Bark, shook his head at the state of Two Bark's fur. "Who was this again?" the doc asked. Shoulder shrug from one of the workers. "Might be Quayle? Ricky?"

Ricky!

"They've removed his ID."

"Looks like that sheep had a run-in with the perimeter, hey?"

The lead man, obviously a doctor, or vet, came over, checked my nose, which, though tender, cracked, still worked well and what a strange odour people have, it's like... a field of wildflowers on fire... horrifying but alluring. "Constock, this one," he said. "Oh yeah?" said the worker who'd opened up the terminal and was replacing a drive or two. "First generation lenses, passable, but the nictitating membrane is clearly artificial. Want some eye drops, hmm?"

"Should we report?"

"It's their job," the doctor said, indicating the sleeping wolves.

Out the corner of my irritated human eye I saw Ricky, Two Bark, Mangy One, watching us. He lowered his head and feigned sleep.

"Alright, software installed, hardware updated, fur removed from fans."

"Let's go topside and breathe again."

And they were gone. First men I'd seen in... first men I'd seen since before the surgery... and those were masked. First faces, first eye-to-eye since Robyn? The falling elevator. The hope.

The niche, said Hog, is that ass-hard seat in a confessional, arsehearts.

In the dark, Two Bark rose from his bed and, claws clicking, nosed up to each sleeping member of his pack. His shoulders tense, his hide twitching, his breathing quick. He lingered over the wolf who'd appeared to be his superior, opened his mouth and began to lick the sleeping wolf's face.

That surprised me.

So much for observational brilliance.

And the superior wolf rose, stretched, moved behind Two Bark and oh dear God, close your eyes, Bones, close your eyes, and mounted him, who steadied himself then moaned while the top dog thrust, mouth open, ears back, and I wasn't sure how that was going on or going in and why the others didn't waken and come to think of it I'd smelled no trick, no drug in the air, so maybe the drug was one of obedience, or the chime Pavlovian, and minutes later they were still going at it.

Unless requested, comes the voice of the brain doctor, his lavender goggles reflecting the courtyard sun, we match sex. You'd think that'd be a fitting punishment, right? Put boy rapist in girl pony. They won't do it, though, unless you x that little box just so. And even then—I backed up as Two Bark and

Top Wolf had staggered too close—it'll happen only if there aren't any same-sex matches.

I didn't recall seeing that x on my sheep sheet.

And there was no reason why any of this should change my half-formed plan.

And as the other wolves began to rouse, yawning, stretching, shaking their heads, Ricky Two Bark and Top Wolf skittered out of sight, did a six-legged, two-backed scurry to a back room and I wondered what strange world I'd entered down here, world of dogs ruling dogs, guards ruling guards. And then there it was again, the sheep sound, unbidden. Eyes turned to me, lingering long. Oh yeah, the match was negative, wasn't it? This sheep is all sheep. Why was I hoping it would be? You can change the goddamned outcome with your mind, Bones, your mind. Hog tapping hard.

Because I thought I could escape.

But I was getting tired of escaping.

Wait, who'd escaped anything? One trap to another, Bones. Life story, huh? If I pounded my head hard enough on the concrete would my brain shake loose and would I experience a short but eternal return to Being, to being Bones, all Bones? One brain adrift in the sub-zero Universe.

Top Wolf returned and a few minutes later Two

Bark, acting casual, slipped to his corner. I took a peek as Two Bark lay down, saw she-wolf parts, now wondered about my powers of seduction as a ram, yes, that's what I am, m'am. All ram. Well, the word had power and promise, if not the body. Right, but ewes stirred something, indeed they did. Close eyes and pretend?

Juggle that, Bones.

The sheep sound again, forlorn this time.

*The Trial of Bones Malone, Part Two*

"Gadgets," says the judge, "make me happy!" My Trial Chair spins, leans forward, backwards, shoots up a few feet, down again, and I feel my stomach bubble into my throat. "Excellent," says the judge, breathing on and polishing the remote control. He then plays with the lights, the guilt meters, the advertising panels—everything seems in order. He blows kisses to the Court Techs in blue uniforms, asks the bailiff to test the back up system, and that too works fine. First pump from the judge. And then the attorneys get harnessed up, play with the controls, some are better than others, mine's a bit jerky with it, nearly flips himself upside down, nearly collides with the prosecution. He comes fast at me, flies by and looks a bit pale, says, "Don't like heights, man!" He stops before colliding with the wall.

There are six members of the prosecution. Their names and Trial Scores are displayed on the guilt meters, five perfect scores and one rookie, a top recruit, a long-legged blonde with a pony tail and thick rimmed glasses. Whistles from the gallery. And then my attorney is on screen, score of 47%, which is higher than I expected, but, wait, his Speed Trial scores are atrocious! "He's oh for eight," I hear through speakers, "and the odds are stacked. Our audience poll shows only a... wow... three percent chance of winning this one. Well, Dolly, I think that's a little pessimistic but I couldn't go more than ten on this myself." Graphic shows skyscrapers, one 100 metres high, the other 10, the other three, image of a kangaroo leaping over the last one.

The judge spins my chair and I'm no longer facing the screens, am facing my attorney and a sheep on a leash. My attorney adjusts the harness's crotch support, says, "Fuck man, did I mention hating Speed Trial? But I got a sheep for you!" He leans forward, whispers, "Love it, love this sheep, desire this sheep, OK?"

"Where'd you get a fucking sheep?"

"Connections, man."

"Is this...?"

"Your Honour," shouts my attorney, "according to Speed Trail rule 74 1.3.1, the defense are allowed one substitute reserve attorney should medical circumstances dictate thusly, and here is my doctor's letter..."

Judge reads... "Oh Christ, night terrors?"

"I haven't slept in a week."

"Then I guess we didn't wake you," laughs the judge.

My attorney smiles weakly.

"OK... so this sheep is your reserve?"

"Yes, Your Honour."

"Fine by me," says the judge.

I'm handed the leash and have the sudden flush of horror that it's this particular sheep that'll hold my brain, that'll churn my food, and I can't look it in the eye. I'm so sorry, is all I can think, because there has to be something there, not just a blank slate, not just an eating and shitting machine. I mean all animals must feel something, fear something, desire something and if they don't think with words, they do *think*, we see it all the time, the pause, the decision, the dog tilting the head, the cat reaching out a paw, the mouse standing, surveying, running for its life. So this sheep, looking at me with one eye, looking at the audience with the other, more range of vision than any human ever had, more sense of peace because hey, what do animals do to pass the time? Birds sit on wires. Cows gaze at trees. Fish undulate with the current. I'm so sorry we're here, I want to say. I can't look you in the eye because I'm a man, and men are terrible, we stick our heads up our asses and say we see God. Poor sheep. How many throats have been cut, how many lambs have been sacrificed in the name of funny hats and lost riddles? And what would the sheep say if the sheep could speak? We like you. You guys are cool.

"Hey, don't cry, man." The bailiff hands me a tissue, I start to blow my nose but see words in blue, *in the final hour we will rush in be prepared xoxo*, and I know it's from Robyn, which sets me crying even harder, which makes the sheep take a couple steps away from me, which makes the man in the Weasel mask snicker, which makes the judge say, "How much did you give him?"

I blow my nose.

My lawyer says, in a tight, clenched-teeth whisper, *It's the drugs, Bones. Now shake it off. Make them laugh. Love the sheep.*

None of this is going to work. The trial begins and I sink lower in my seat, let my body react passively as the chair responds to each command the judge toggles, he's having fun, for a while my head flops left, right, as if my brain has already started to shut down, disconnect, saying it's for the best, it has to be this way, it'll be too painful if we stay in touch but it's been wonderful, truly, you guys are the best organ buds ever. Introductions are made, the jury is of course the audience in attendance and paid subscribers, and as per court rules the victims and those testifying wear Masks of the Afflicted, thus Bunny is her beloved Harvey, and this makes sense, but the gang, really? They are afflicted? My chair shoots up, I hear the judge's booming voice, "Bones Malone do you understand the consequences of the immorality of your existence, or something like that?" The poor sheep is choking, front feet off the ground, so I let go of the lead and the sheep goes a bit crazy, yeah. "Order, silence!" Sheep is running through the audience, the coffee-scented jurists, and already the guilt meters are in the red zone, 90%. Fuck, can't I just go back to bed, do you really need me here?

A brief introduction regarding the criminality in my DNA, then the prosecution show video stills identifying Bones at various places. There I am with the gang (their faces blurred with swirls) at Froggies, at Ye Olde Bear, sleeping on Hog's mother's couch. There I am smiling, cutting up cardboard for the mock-up. There I am sitting on a park bench, head resting on fist, a lovely black and white photo, actually. Oh, but across from the bench is the Carat Top. And there I am leaving the car with a swirl-faced Hog, there I am slapping swirly Goose on the sidewalk and it stops. Wouldn't want to give everything away now would we?

A bailiff returns the sheep to me. My hand idly pets it.

My lawyer objects to the slide show, saying "It's really fucking boring. Isn't this a Speed Trial?" And the guilt meter falls. "He's good," I say to the sheep.

But up next are the videos, though not after more coffee is served and a continental breakfast. My attorney slips out of his harness and says, "We're down to 71%, OK, OK. But are you going to love the sheep? Want some toast?" I try to oblige, have a sip of coffee, but find my head and stomach are not in agreement. "It's beginning already," I mutter. "It's irreconcilable."

Across the way Goose-as-Weasel taps his foot, he's restless, wants action. Weasel-as-Hog is making origami birds and giving them to female jurists. Hog, as Goose, is motionless, hands folded on the table. Maybe they're all impostors, I think. Maybe the gang has been unganged, gagged or hung but the way Weasel-mask jerks back, yes I swear I hear a honking. "She can't eat this, right?" My lawyer with a croissant and jam and I say, "It's grains sort of but I don't think she's hungry and what exactly do you want me to do?"

"Is your heart not in this, Bones?" he says. "I just want you to act weird with the sheep, make the audience feel uncomfortable, you know?"

I tell him I can't see how that'll help me with the jury.

"They're sleepy, their brains aren't working right, confuse them, man."

"You mean, like, lick my lips, eye the sheep with..."

"Yes! Exactly!"

"You've lost every Speed Trial..."

"Because I tried! So I'm not trying this time. Trust me."

"No."

"Bones..."

"You're insane."

Next, the videos, more of the same. We're on

the move, but something's not right. Yes, that's the gang, yes, that's us drinking, yes that's us kicking the plexiglass door at the Carat Top, in the dark, then running, but hey that never happened! We discussed that, we didn't do it. Whoa. And there I am, leaning back, saying the word scheme over and over, scheme, scheme, scheme, and swirl-faced Weasel is laughing saying, stop it, you're scaring me. Audience chuckle. And there I am cleaning my gun, cocking it, aiming it at the camera, Bang bang, I say. Gasps from the audience.

I can't bring myself to even touch the sheep now.

I try to get my lawyer's attention, but he's wrapped up in it too.

And then the fateful robbery, the car racing from the Mother Lair, the music aggressive, pounding, lyrics crawling with bad intention, shoot and rape, rape and shoot, kill the bastids, take the loot, and a shadow of a fist, mine, and Goose is out of it (gasp), we place him at the door. And then video of Weasel, trying to sneak in, desperate, swearing, calling for help, and then saying, Run, run for your lives, it's Bones, he's evil, man, freaky evil, and Harvey calling Bunny. But it's too late, Hog is in the building, Hog runs to Weasel and sits on him, yes, but is weeping, disconsolate, saying, What should we do he's a madman, a madman, and I look over to the Goose-masked Hog sitting across and he's motionless, hands folded. Harvey shouts, We have called the police, they will protect us from this monster, but if I have to die protecting you all, I will, goshdang it. Bunny is hysterical, pointing her gun, saying, How do I use this, do I aim and pull the trigger like this? Aw, man, really? Does anyone believe this shit? My lawyer, swaying in his harness, has his palm over his mouth. The prosecution hang in a circle, are holding hands. I hear the judge's breathing and then a honk. I look to Goose-as-Weasel.

If I throw myself on the sheep, grab her face and kiss her muzzle, how long till the Constriction Cloth takes hold?

And here I come into the scene, arms upraised, saying, The Lord tells me one of you will die today who will it be? Hog gets off Weasel hands me his coat, says, Leave the innocent, take me, I deserve it. And Weasel leaps up and says, No, me, I'm just a lowly pickpocket, can I have a kiss? And Bunny shouts Do I pull the trigger, bang, bang? What do I do?

And Bones.

Bones grabs the gun.

The video stops, the prosecution swoop low

over the audience and behind these flying men of law the guilt meters are flaring, 99%, fires of hell, sizzling sounds, a sheep turning on a spit, and a voice, booming, it's the lead prosecutor, saying, "At this point the Mephistophelian accused shot the camera" (boo) "but we hired a reliable neutral party to recreate the events as we believe they took place, and with Your Honour's permission..."

The judge doesn't even speak, clicks play on his remote, the lights dim, the guilt meters fade to black, the video loads and the sheep at my side, sensing my distress, she comes to me, like a dog she stands and sets her hooves on my lap, such a nice, nice sheep. And as I pet her gentle head she eats my toast and jam.

*The Parable of Weasel and the Fly*

It plays in my mind like a short film, cracked and burnt and jumpy in a theatre so dark only the glint of eyes and teeth is seen. It starts with a voice, Weasel's, breathing hard, he's woken from a nightmare, he's up in bed, he rushes down a hallway and slams through my door.

He fumbles through the room, clicks a button

and a dim lamp is glowing.

Are you awake, are you awake, Bones?

Oh fuck, man, I had it again, the dream, the goddamn dream, he says.

Yeah, he's back, man, he says.

And this time it was so fucking great (almost weeping), so fucking perfect, because we had this band, the gang had a band, I was lead singer, did this awesome howling shit (howls), fuck. And Hog was on bass, man, he was amazing, slapping out funky, Jesus he was good. And you, man, you played this freaky guitar, it was like an inside-out guitar and you could put your hands in the body and there were these fleshy knobs, you know? But it sounded like a symphony in an underwater cathedral, oh man. Loved it. And Goosey, he was on drums.

And you know what, we were playing in a church.

Ah, fuck man. That sound, it's in my head, it's the shit no one's ever made but it's, it's, it's what soul fucking music should be, pure and totally fucked, hey? Ah man, I can't believe it's gone.

Yeah, I know, Bones, I know. I hate that too.

(Punches the bed.)

So we start playing, it's a song called "Beef of Rife," starts like a motherfucking seizure, all jammed to shit, then opens up with sweet spaces of sound, like an angel orgy, and just as it's about to *soargasm*, man, fuck, Goose, on drums, he screams, but I think sure, this is part of the song, and he keeps screaming but it's getting on my nerves, you know, he's pushing it too far, and he's not even keeping rhythm anymore, he's like, five bars ahead.

And how the hell do I know that, Bones? What the fuck?

What the fuck do I know about music? Bars?

Fucking dreams, man.

They fuck with ya, they say ha ha, you could be so much more but you're going die having only scratched the useless surface.

I hear this screech, man, this sound like a stylus over vinyl, but it's words, too, it's saying *beet of riiiite* like it's possessed and fuck, yeah man, it's the fly. Again! There's no more Goose it's the fucking fly on drums! But it's Goose, too, you know? And I step back and say whoa shit dudes y'all got flies in ya! And you guys are like yeah, so? And the fly, just sits there, somehow holding the drumsticks like it's denying all laws of fucking physics, it just wants to play. Boom boom, boom boom, let's go.

No fucking flies in the band, I shout.

But you guys (breathing fast again), you don't

care. Let's go, let's go.

No, fuck, I say. No! Last time he flew out of my fucking girlfriend's crotch and he's in all my fucking food. Fuck off, fly!

Boom boom, boom boom.

Then everybody starts to play, I'm in tears but no one gives a shit and I feel pressured, so I'm trying to sing but when I get to the chorus the fly takes over *beer of riiile, beer of riiile* and it's not keeping time at all! So I throw the fucking microphone at the goddamn filthy fucking church wall and yeah, oh boy, that stops everyone.

Give me a beat, four-four time, fly.

The fly starts to play but soon we're all looking at each other, making faces. Fly can't play for shit.

So I think, I'll reason with the fucker, though part of me is thinking, bad idea, dude.

You can't play if you can't keep time, fly.

Boom boom, boom boom.

What the fuck's that, fly?

Boom boom, boom BOOM.

That all?

Boomboom boomboom boomboomboomboomboom.

I start clapping my hands, say follow along, fly (whispering), a sweet-ass cheerleader rhythm, and he can't fucking do it! He's getting pissed too, buzzing away screeching out *been on riiime* and I say *beef of riiife* and the fucker goes nutso, what the fuck, gets bigger and bigger and ffffuck that's ugly, bout the size of fat fucking pigeon and I just want to splash its fucking guts on the wall but the thought, man, I gag, there's like flies in my throat, maggots even, and in the corner over there it's Goose, he's all rotting skinbag and more flies and I puke, man, and...

OK, I'll spare you details (shudders).

It's just, I know it's there, in me, that fly. I can feel it.

It's quiet for a moment, people eat their popcorn in the blackness, Weasel sits at the base of the bed, legs sprawled, face sweating, while I'm sitting up picking sleep from my eyes, yawning.

The soundtrack is running water and something dragging a limb.

Weasel looks up, grabs my wrist. Know what you said, man? Do you remember? Oh yeah, *my* dream. You said, fuck. Always so rational. I had the fucker, eh? Had his prickly little squishy fly body up against the wall, could feel him squirming, smelled like dirty armpits, could feel cold greasy death in the room. I'm ending this, fly. Didn't feel an infant's tit of sorrow, either.

But then, all profound-like, you say, and your guitar does this dream shit in the background, you say, Flies aren't like us, Weasel. They experience the world in a different time. A day to a fly is like a month to us. It's neurochemical, Weasel. The signal journey to a fly's brain is so much shorter than it is for us, and it's the same for the response. To catch a fly, you have to anticipate where the fly will be, you have to predict the future. So to play with a fly, we have to play into the future, or, in your case, sing to the future. Can you do that, Weasel?

But, but look what it did to Goose!

And... and it wants to sing! I'm the singer!

I can't sing in future time, man!

Anyway, Bones, fuck, the fly slipped away, went back to the drum kit. We could have been great, you know? Famous. But the fucking fly had to be in everything. Why does the fly have to be in everything?

I'm sick of it, Bones.

I'm sick of it.

The film ends and the credits scroll. The gang, I see, have done almost everything, from casting to key grip. The fly doubled as make-up artist, and Hog's Mother was music consultant. In bed, I lie awake, run my fingers through my hair, feel the scars. In the back of my skull the aurora of a migraine is flickering over black mountains and I reach for my medication, but it's not there. I shuffle toward the washroom, knowing I need to hurry, the window is open but will close soon, stars shoot across the sky, and my movement across the room makes papers on the table flutter.

*Sheep Who Run with the Wolves*

I had a dog once, when I was still in grade school. It was a small dog, black and brown, a terrier of some sort, and it followed me everywhere, as dogs are wont to do. It would wait outside, in the schoolyard, ignoring strangers, looking up to the windows, sometimes sleeping under a bench, sometimes on the bench. It never barked.

The dog, which was named Georgie, which I suspect was the name given by the previous owners (yes, this was a used dog), lived for a few years, died while I was at summer Bible camp, a summer camp where I broke my wrist falling from a tree. Wait, pushed from a tree. Tell a story often enough and you will believe the story of the apple tree and the highest, juiciest apple and reaching, reaching (boy you sure loved apples) and crack the limb goes. Told that story so often I've forgotten the name of the pusher, but I remember his curly brown hair, stocky kid. Jesus, wasn't Hog was it?

Georgie had an accident. We buried him in the woods.

Where?

Don't go looking, you'll fall into that hole too.

So for years I believed Georgie had been running, chasing a mole, then thump, fell into a hole, broke a paw (like me), waited, whimpered, starved to death, and then was buried in that same hole, except wasn't buried well, and the soil was like quicksand and one day I'd run, fall in, legs sinking down and bare feet touching the decaying body. Worms between my toes.

Well, here the question was, could the man in my sheep command the dog in the guards? I admit, this was a eureka moment, the thought that all I had to do was carry myself like a man and... that was as long as that thought lasted. Not only did they have wolf-to-sheep advantage, they also had guard-to-prisoner advantage.

But in any case, I kept standing.

They kept watching.

The sheep in me was getting increasingly

nervous.

Two Bark, Ricky, he was the key.

With Georgie, I would say come, then clap, and Georgie would leap along, and I would say you're a furry frog and Georgie would yip and yap as if saying dog, dog, not frog. Before Ricky inhabited that body, there was a dog's heart, well, there still was a dog's heart but I wasn't foolish enough to think anything of that. What's in the hindbrain of a wolf? Nothing good, I imagined. But still.

I bleated loudly this time, then did the only I thing I could think of to get their minds off eating me: I turned my ass toward them and shat, which felt good, which also had the effect of another one-on-one with Two Bark. But good God they weren't going to make him eat?

Yeah.

So I put my mind on other things, turned my head and tried to ignore the slurping sounds, the gagging sounds, thought of Georgie some more, thought of my parents, my brother, the family that went from completely fucking normal to utterly fucking bizarre in one drizzly afternoon when the doorbell rang, when my mother said, You're back, are ya? I went out, I remember, because the man at the door gave me the creeps, talked too softly, like a bird with brain damage, and I walked in the rain, down to a culvert, yes, threw stones at tadpoles, tried to catch a dragonfly, hid in the culvert when the rain came harder, shouted out words, played with the echo, knew that no one would feed Georgie while I was away so hours later I returned, a long walk through a forested lot, saw the bird brain's car leaving and, soaked, entered quietly through the back door, heard excited whispers and thought we've just won a lot of money, or someone's died, yes, and I fed Georgie, dished out dogfood and my mother, hearing this noise, came around the corner and screamed Jesus where the hell did you come from, and my father said We can't use that language anymore and my mother covered her mouth and a month later we'd moved out, joined the commune, and a month after that my brother, twice my age, was exiled for heinous behaviour, and not too much longer after that, I must admit, I too was on the run, fleeing the cult's 'Gatherers' and living on the streets. Maybe a year?

I, Bones the Sheep, am a product of the Church of Final Friday. We didn't know when the apocalypse would arrive, but we were betting on a Friday, so every Friday we'd prepare ourselves for the Hereafter, a Hereafter in which, I was told, Georgie would come back and not only run at my side, but would also talk with me, in fact all the animals would talk, which freaked me out, perhaps more so than dressing in white and lying in bed for hours on end each Friday, the room dark, Father singing, Mother sighing.

Two Bark was growling at me.

I bleated, bleated as loud as I could, bleated in his face, threatened to shit again, started gagging, then bleated in a very inhuman, or unsheeply way. A horrible sound and it worked, the guards started barking and Richard "Two Bark" Quayle took my lead in his mouth and to the back room we went, and then to a room behind that one.

So, can we have a little chat, Ricky? No? I know you're pissed, but get over it. I'm not the one who made you eat shit, OK? Slow down. We need to stop so I can scratch this out but Ricky wouldn't let me stop, led me deeper into the darkness and I started to think I hear cheering, I'm heading back to the square, Moll and Fergus await, the horns are sharper than ever and a net's been placed over the top, no one can leap in, no one can leap out and I ran forward and headbutted Ricky, headbutted him again but he leaped out of the way and had me by the throat, on my back, and that was the end of that.

Georgie would never have done this.

My little legs kicked and I thought this is the end, a stupid way to die, my heroics will never be told, I'll be a footnote, hoofnote, endnote. I waited for a final tightening, teeth sinking in, but after a few seconds I realized it wasn't happening and all shit breath wanted to do was calm me down, because I did kind of lose it there, with the head butting.

So, lying on my back in a room of empty cages, I tried to calm myself. I closed my eyes, thought of Georgie running alongside me, it was a wide field and we were running for the river, that was calming, yes, we'd frolic, or something, try to catch fish, explore farther downstream but Georgie says, The people are there, and I see them, through the trees, dressed in white, floating on the water, the sun sparkling off the waves, this is the end times and so I run the other way but Georgie keeps on heading to the river, I call him but damn, the Fridays hear me, sit up on the water and, No Georgie, no, I call but I don't turn around, I run, have been running forever, run like when I left that night, hopped into my brother's car, which he'd stolen, which he'd crash and burn in later that night.

He's not long for this world, my mother said.

But *we* are eternal.

Lack of oxygen, perhaps, or a dizzying result of lying on one's back, but I came to in the cell and Two Bark was gone. Maybe I've only ever had one escape in me, and that came years ago. The robbery was a joke, the trial a fiasco, the surgery nearly killed me and here I am, Bones, alone, yes, oh that's better, Bones Alone, yes, that's who I've always been. Bones Alone. Bones Alone in the dark cell of his sheep's head but was it ever any different before?

I bleated softly, put my nose between the iron bars, Water, please, hello, and a little bread? I'm just an innocent lamb, can't you see? Hello? Anyone?

*The Trial of Bones Malone, Part Three*

I would find out later, sitting by my lawyer in his hospital bed, his various limbs suspended and his body-cast lacking a single autograph (no, I would prefer that you didn't, Bones), that the video was damning evidence, how I sauntered in like a cowboy, casually shot the camera, casually grabbed the handgun from Bunny, and casually (yes, I get it) put Bunny's own gun to her blue-haired head. "Everyone screamed," my lawyer would tell me, "'No, don't shoot Bunny', and you laughed, said

'OK', and"—casually, I know—"shot poor Harvey in the soft belly. Her beloved! He fell kind of funny, Bones, and you pointed the gun and laughed, laughed, made the others laugh with you. It was awful."

In the courtroom, however, that video never fully loads.

The sheep senses things first, looks up and follows an arcing across the ceiling, and before I can even wonder what the heck it is, there's a holler and another something soars across the room. A small explosion and the sheep bounds into the air, hits the ground and topples and all hell breaks loose. Before the judge can yell for security, smoke canisters have filled the room with a pink and green fog and the lights returning to full power only make things worse. In the chaos, for now shouts can be heard above the frightened audience, the flying attorneys become entangled and start falling from the sky like suit-and-tie angels. My chair, meanwhile, wobbles and spins while the judge bellows out commands from above, "We're under attack, everyone stay calm, hide under your seats," and above the shouting, a sheep, bleating.

I hear my lawyer scream in pain, he pleads with the tall bailiff to help him but the bailiff is at my side, is undoing my arm straps, and lo there's a fashion model in a black bodysuit freeing my foot straps, helping me up, escorting me into the bright, blinding fog as another angel falls from heaven just missing the bailiff, and I hear, "This way, this way," and then, "No, here, here," and then fuck, we're falling over audience chairs and "My fucking shin," I hear the bailiff cry, and "The sheep, we have to get the sheep" and my lithe rescuer, whose sharp hip my hand was holding, is gone. People are spilling over one another and shots are heard and the bailiff, still at my side but now unable to stand, he says, "Go on without me, run, Bones," but Jesus, I'm tripping over chairs and people and how many fucking smoke canisters did they need? Yes there are shots flying over my head, security with piercing lights, the judge still hollering commands and the sound of a sheep and a woman's voice, Robyn's voice, saying, "Oh my God she's bleeding." But I'm running, yes, in the clear now, I think, the door, the exit should be right here and oh fuck, I'm flying having tripped on a body and I smack my head hard on something that shouts in pain and it's my goddamn lawyer I've tripped over, so I'm nowhere near the fucking exit, and before I can get up and run there's a tightening, as if I've caught my clothing on a hook that's pulling me out of the misty sea but then everything tightens, arms, chest, legs, crotch as the Constriction Cloth takes hold, the question mark on my back shrinking to a grim certainty. I can't move, can hardly breathe.

The judge looms over me, clicks a control, "How tight do you want it, huh?"

"Shut that sheep up," he shouts.

Portable fans are brought in, the smoke clears, medical personal attend to dozens of trampled audience members and six fallen lawyers. The seventh lawyer droops silently, swaying, his harness a hangman's noose. The bailiff, he with the bloodied shin, is manhandled by security, cuffed and frogmarched out of the courtroom shouting, "I will die for my ethics! Long live PASCAL!"

"It's a got a broken leg," someone calls from the upper part of the courtroom. "And there's something written on its back. In green."

The judge says, "Well, what?"

"It, um, looks like... FETA... FETA... I can't read it."

"Bring it here," says the judge, who then turns to me and says, "Too tight? " I nod, gasp for air. My lawyer moans something about my rights and the trial not being completed and the jumper loosens a little. The sheep, eyes glassy, arrives cradled in the blue arms of a court tech.

"Is this your co-counsel?"

"Huh?" says my lawyer

"Did you write this?" asks the judge.

"Fuck no, man," says my lawyer.

"FETAFFY. Can you tell my why your co-counsel has FETAFFY written on him, or her?"

"Help me, please," says my lawyer before passing out.

I'm helped up, am handcuffed because the Constriction Cloth will need time to recover. There's no sign of Robyn in the room, or any of the other PETABBY forces. Broken chairs, papers, shoes. Must've been hell for her to leave the sheep behind.

Slowly they lower the hung lawyer.

"Better lawyer than jury," someone snickers.

From his hospital bed my lawyer would tell me the rest of it. "They had to go on without you, Bones," set it up in the judge's quarters, jury pulled off the street, the prosecution down to three, the defense a count-appointed law student who had been lost in the basement, but was the only person they could find in time. "You have three hours for Speed Trial, Bones, and they had ten minutes left. The student did the best she could but knew nothing about the case and had no time to review notes. Her defense was that you were on nasty drugs on thus not responsible for whatever it was you had done, unless it was selling drugs, in which case you wanted to change your plea to guilty. I have the video if you want it. She's convincing but rather homely. Don't they have a cure for that?"

In the room, the light falling, clouds rolling in, I ask why I wasn't notified, surely I could have done a better job than a lost girl but my lawyer just waves me away, foolish question, mutters something about opening a barber shop, the steady need for cutting hair, the flow of customers.

"The witnesses, the video recreation, the evidence, your gang's testimony, your shrink's testimony, and organized crime links? You had no chance, Bones. We tried. Let it go. Sentencing is—ow, could you lift my leg a little?—a few weeks from now. Enjoy the days, Bones. Get a hobby. We go through life forgetting the little things, don't we? The fit of a good pair of shoes, or standing and stretching in the morning. A hot bath. Dancing a jig. We forget and the next thing you know you're falling, about to break every bone in your body, about to die, or be crippled, and what for? Justice? What the hell is justice? What the hell is justice when you can say no, that's not justice anymore, this is, or this is. Let's make new laws. Let's play more games. I tell you, Bones, there should be only one law out there, one big motherfucking law that says thou shall not suspend acrofuckingphobic lawyers from wires! Jesus! I knew that was a fucked up idea. Constock? Sorry, but I like it. Play Prison? Fantastic idea. Pay Prison? Tried and true. But what the hell is going on? I mean, it's like prison is the place to be. There are, I swear, line-ups, waiting lists, people on their knees begging to be punished. What have we done? We, we need to break the world apart, my friend, we need to give each and every sane and insane person an island, and a beach umbrella, and maybe a talking robot companion. Aw, never mind. Listen to me, Bones, rambling like that old fart you shot in the belly. Sorry, that the wife shot. Just rambling. I'm losing my mind, Bones..."

But it's me whom the guards drag away.

*Cell Mates*

On the third day after his surgery, Sylvester Moll, the first publicly acknowledged winner of the Constock Sweepstakes, died. Heard it on the radio that morning, coming from a car parked outside my window: *Bad news for the Constock program today, as its original and likely most deserving manimal croaked overnight. Yes, Moll has bought the farm, apparently due to massive systemic rejection of his horrible brain. Well, it's as if that pig's body knew better than all those boys and girls who decided to take a ride in his funmobile, eh?*

The doctors assured us that this was only a small setback, that the Constock in question must have somehow tampered with his ARM, the anti-rejection module that would have been implanted along with his brain. They offered no clues on how this could be done, seeing that the ARM was located under the skull. Perhaps he thought it was a tracking device and scratched it out? Essentially, the brain, attacked on all sides, explodes, said my shrink when I brought up my fears. And that can't be pleasant, he stressed. Out the ears and eyes, you know? He pointed to the areas of cranial egress while grimacing. But it shouldn't happen, so don't worry about it. And anyway, he didn't die, did he?

Every small headache and you begin to wonder.

Food, water, go without these and your brain begins to hurt. And what if the ARM isn't properly loaded? Or what if it is made to expire? What if there's a lab technician who's taking the law into her own hands? Oh, you can see her, can't you? Works late, has short, curly hair, never wears make-up, a permanent scowl, has cats and dogs and rats and has no friends.

Don't leave the prisoner Alone with his brain for too long.

Something during the night set the guards barking, howling.

And through the howling I waited for Two Bark to return, paced my cell and tried not to think about my brain, which wasn't working, because a headache becomes your universe and try to escape, no, no, no you can't. Pacing, resting, needing to accept that they *weren't going to feed me* but the sheep in me wasn't letting that happen. Just sit, and rest, try to sleep some, and nope, up on my feet, my nose between the bars, bah, bah, give me some *goddamn stop it now*. Yes, sit, rest dammit, sit the fuck back down, you're giving me such a fucking headache, stop pacing, and then this urge to slam my head into the walls, the bars, knock my brain loose and stomp the fucker to a moronic pulp. I'm not an animal! Give me some goddamn oats!

Your sheep body will try you, but you must remain in control. Pause. Tugs beard. Or not. I've been fascinated with Zen lately, hmm. Well, this is what I suggest. Hmm, wait.

Howling, as if there was a full fucking moon.

This went on for some time, and the more reasonable part of my mind, the one that wasn't trying to make my hind legs go fore and my forelegs go aft, was telling me, You're having a breakdown of some sort, Bones, this has happened before, like when you were abandoned at the rodeo when you were five, an hour of wandering, sobbing, panicking, but then you found them, in the parking lot, arguing, the car idling. This is a very human thing and not brain rejection at all, Bones.

A cockroach skitters under you, skitters under the bars.

Yes, said the shrink, but perhaps only as a last resort. Yes, this is what I think you should do, if you find you're troubled, that is. I believe it's important for you to remain human, because human is the highest level of intelligence, for lack of a better word. Although (finger pointed), studies on cetaceans have certainly revealed intriguing results. But I digress, and your time is short.

Yes, try to stay human, he says, but if it's not working, do let go.

My sheep sounds were lost in the howling.

And finally my body gave out. There was a

stinging in my throat, where Two Bark had grabbed me. My nose throbbed, my head pulsed, my spine stiffened and my legs and hips shuddered. I lay down and watched the cockroach at eye level, watched it scurry back toward me, it too trying to negotiate its way through the madness. I named it Weasel's Daughter, told it to bring me the key of the gate and as much dewy grass as it could carry. Its antennae twitched. It skittered toward the control room and I closed my eyes, saw patterns of geometric light, red, purple, yellow, saw the number eight rotating on its axis, black, red, blue, and then it was an ant crawling out of my line of sight. The floor smelled of dog piss.

Was there a key?

No, the mutt held no key. And the unhappy cockroach was returning.

So I drifted in and out of awareness, in the cell, dreams floating up only to fall back, sift through the concrete floor, enlighten the odd worm with an image, a shoe's sole, perhaps. Drifted till morning when I was woken by the grunting, the scritch of claws coming near, and I feigned death. I saw the shadow before I saw the light, but the shadow told all: leave men to their own devices and they act like dogs. Shuffling my way were Top Dog and

Ricky, ready for their morning routine of hidden humping, their eyes glazed. The cockroach watched from afar, wondering why these hideous mountains of flesh and fur would go through such trouble. Lay an egg, would ya? They came scatter-shuffling through one room, into the cell block, a spasm of shadows, certainly trying to keep their grunting low, wouldn't want to wake the other guards, wouldn't want this to get out. One summer day, Weasel and I were watching a bull mount a cow, side of the road, and Weasel flicked his cigarette into the field, said he hoped it would burn, save them all from the utter shame. That's why them fucking whales, he would say on the way home, literally them fucking whales—that's why they went to sea, Bones. Ever seen elephants, or rhinos doing it, man? You are inelegant, elephant!

Sea because?

Flippers have grace, man! And hands, too. But paws and hooves?

I stared at my hooves as Top Dog and Ricky scuffled closer to the cage. Jesus. So close, in fact, that they came up against the bars. Christ. I didn't move, not even when Ricky's muzzle was over my head, growling deep in his throat as Top Dog thrust, thrust, causing the bars to rattle. I didn't move when a drop of drool landed on my nose. I didn't move when I thought Top Dog might play it safe and pull out and shower me with wolf jism. And I didn't move when the thrusting against the bars seemed to unlatch the door. Yes, Ricky's furry face was pressing against some kind of mechanism, causing it to latch, unlatch, latch again, and so on.

But I did move when it opened just enough that I could slip my slender hoof in between, and what happened next, though pure accident, was surely elegant:

A powerful, cumming thrust, and the cell door, under weight of orgasm, swung wide and master and mange fell forward, into the cell while I, quick little ruminant that I am, prey to wolves and prison guards, escaped, pushed the door shut with my head and gave a surprised little sheep laugh. *Bah ha!*

Yeah, I planned that.

Oh, you could see their panic through the glaze. How will we ever explain this? They looked to the control room, wanted to bark, but were still locked in their lumpy embrace and would be for a while. What have you done to us, tasty sheep? Richard "Two Bark" Quayle, still supporting his superior, lowered his head. His superior panted, eyes searching the cell for solutions. And the cockroach led the way, led me deeper into the complex, away from the control room, down past empty cell after empty cell, until I came to a glowing red sign, and a ramp, and here the cockroach and I said our farewells. *You haven't much time, gigantic fur thing*, said the cockroach, *so go up and slip under the door and be with the great light, but be careful, because no one will love you.*

A salute!

Before leaving, setting off an alarm when my hoof depressed the door pedal, which I by chance stepped on while trying to turn the knob with my teeth, I noticed that some clever person had changed the EXIT sign to read REXIT.

Once again, I was free.

*They removed the brain from the pig, expecting to study it. Seemed such a normal brain, all pale pink and convoluted, a little swollen but not so bad, really. Tests showed that there was activity, and lots of it. Do we study, or do we try again? They gently washed the brain in a solution of energizing sea salts and essential flower oils and kept all eyes on the monitor. This brain is dreaming, for sure! One of them shouted that. I think it's dreaming it's a baby, in a tub, but I can't prove that. They dipped rods into the warm bath and shocked the brain, just to see what would happen. Increased activity on the monitor. The dream has changed, I think. I think the tub is full of burning embers and that baby is dancing. Up the voltage. Wow. That baby has just leaped from the tub and is a young boy, running through a field, his manhood growing.*

*Quick, quick, bring another pig!*


### Run On Sentencing

I don't see my lawyer again. In my windowless cell, lying in bed, a bed that I could lie in for the rest of my life, I challenge my mind to find a way out, for there must be a way out, but my mind does nothing, for it too is lying lazily, thinks, I'll be fine, probably. My legs twitch, my fingers drum on the wall. I sit up, I lie back down, replay the trial in my head, smack myself for not studying the exit routes, not holding on tighter to Robyn as she tried to lead me out. But where would I be? On the run, perhaps running at this very moment, limping, with a bullet in my leg, and Robyn, no Wren, the leader, dead, shot dead, half his fair-haired head blown onto Robyn's lap, poor Robyn, she'll never be the same.

Or you're a new man, Bones, you're Federico Falanges from Roma, you sell racing cars, learn your

Italian fast. And gesture lots. OK?

They make you practice flirting with Robyn. Too subtle! More confidence!

Make you practice stick shift and catcalling.

Fantasy is the last outpost of sanity, you must know. It thinks it can hide there, wander out onto the ice then run back inside, so daring, what a thrill, but what sanity doesn't know is madness is impatient, and it grows, it'll surround your little fantasy outpost and the next time you open the door...

The cell is secluded, smallest sounds are heard. Echoey unlocking, footsteps, two people, one a heavy-hoofed guard, the other a shuffling, awkward, crippled ballerina. Morning came and they told me I'd have a visitor, would see my new lawyer and that she'd bring news of my case. They acted like they already knew my fate, the smirking guards. It's as if the ability to smirk, or sneer, it's what this new government looks for in public employees.

"Look up, prisoner. Here's your saviour."

It's my new lawyer, all five feet high of her, bowlegged under a tight grey skirt, ash-dull hair swept to one side and sticking out as if she styled it in a wind tunnel. It's the new thing, I guess, have seen it here and there, so that means she's trying.

She has horse teeth, too, but that doesn't stop her from smiling. And she's excited to see me, a thrill shakes her body, shakes the computer cradled to her ample chest. She does smell nice.

Profanities from the rotted mouth of Goose.

"He's harmless," says the guard, and my new lawyer, with a smile, says, "I know." He lets her in and she rushes to my side, sits on the bed, and says, "It's such a pleasure to meet you, Bones, can I call you that? You are in good hands with me, I promise you. I mean I don't have much experience but I'm a hard worker and... yes, I do all my research and you know, I care, I really care about my clients. Of which you're the first. But you know I imagine, no I know that I will always care about my clients as if they were my own children. I mean I don't have children yet, but I imagine I'd be a great mom, because I've always been very detail oriented and, and a hard worker. So!"

The guard leaves us.

She says her name is Drosophila, which is an odd name, she admits, but it's Greek, not that she's from Greece, nor her parents, who spent too much time laboratories. "But they always loved the classics, you know? A name should be classic! Unless it's a great sobriquet like yours, of course." She sets the computer down and takes off her flat-soled shoes and brings her bare feet up on the bed, looks around, says, "This place isn't so bad, you know? I mean it's clean, the bed is comfy. A bit hard is better for your back anyway, right? I bet some people would pay for a bit of R and R here." She laughs, then turns to me and tells me I have such kind eyes, very innocent eyes, and says it was my eyes that drew her to this case.

"Didn't they find you in the basement?" I say.

"Oh, well, yeah—that was hilarious. I'd been lost in those archives for hours! Told my mother I'd get there early and then meet her for supper but my God midnight came and then it was *really* late and I couldn't even remember what I was looking for and next thing some lunatic comes running down the hallway asking if I wanted to make a few bucks and I thought, huh, this is some kind of pervert but I guess it was legit. And I'm so sorry but I had no time to prepare. I mean I was told what happened and by the time I was in the judge's quarters I'd thought of a defense, because why else would someone hurt an old person if not for drugs?

"But when I saw your eyes…"

"You knew I didn't do it."

"Well now I won't go so far as to say that, the

judge did decide otherwise, and he's a smart one, and maybe because you know I think a part of me is thrilled that you might be some crazed killer with… those… innocent eyes. But right you say you didn't do it?"

"Didn't you read the transcripts, watch the video, talk to my previous lawyer?"

She plays with a button on her blouse, a simple, navy blue, short-sleeved blouse and she reminds me of a girl I knew, a girl who'd developed too quickly, who went around showing all the boys and girls her breasts as if they were birds that had landed on her one day. Soon that button would pop off then the others would follow, hitting the cell wall and landing in an unfamiliar constellation. "Yeah," she says, "I did, honestly, but you know, I don't retain well. I mean you're reading, right, trying cram everything in but your mind drifts away, you start thinking about what it's like to be on the other side, to have been abused and bullied so much that you hate the world, hate hugs and hate baby animals. But yeah, yes, I read everything so I'm sure it's in there somewhere!"

"Just, listen, Dru…"

"Everyone calls me Sophi."

"Does it matter?"

"What?"

"That I didn't do it?"

She scrunches her face, which oddly makes her pretty, and I wonder if she'd do me, right here, on the bed that she says is great for the back, and when will I get the chance again, six months since the barmaid and how long till I'm Constock, so this is what I have to do, act now, and she puts her hand on my arm and says, "No, it really is too late you know? I'm sorry but today I'm just a messenger. I hope you don't shoot me. Oh. God. I'm so Sorry, that was a terrible joke, can't believe I just said that."

She closes her blouse button.

"You must hate me right now," she says, fingers making circles on the computer by her side.

I stand, draw an imaginary square on the cell wall, the wall I assume is facing the outside. I was blindfolded when they brought me in, don't know the neighbourhood. "If I stepped through this square, how far down would I fall?" I ask her, and she's puzzled, laughs nervously, so I say, "This is a window, what do I see today? Pissing rain? Sleet?"

"Um, dirt," she says. "We're below ground."

"How long did you study law?"

"Oh," she sits up straight, puts the computer on her lap. "Yeah I studied for, well I took the six-month intensive and then the three-month practical and then I apprenticed for a week."

"It was hard?"

"Oh I stayed up late so many nights studying!"

"The nation needs attorneys."

"We still don't have enough!"

"I have to get out of here, Sophi. If you care for me, you'll find a way. You don't know what awaits me."

She opens the computer on her lap, says, "Oh but I do! That's why I'm here. Sit, sit," she says, patting the bed. "Sit and we'll watch it together. Oh, and here." She reaches into a paper bag and hands me a little something, a lemon tart in a small box, says, "A little birdy told me you like these, so I hope you do." And what can I do but thank her, my left hand has the beginning of a tremor and my life without tarts flashes before me, and now the image of farm animals is on her computer screen, and maybe things start to become real, for as mad as this society is, it certainly is real. But I have a lemon tart.

"I'll try not to cry this time," she says.

I eat the lemon tart as the video plays, as the video shows the judge from my case explaining that "Due to terrorist threats we have decided to sentence the criminal *in absentia*, per rule bla bla

bla, and here are the witnesses, and someone turn that music off." The judge's papers are out of order, he leafs through and says, "What the hell," turning one upside down and flinging it away, and then, "Alright, yes, it has been decided that the criminal is, uh, yes to be delivered to the CCC, where he will be prepared for his transition to, yada yada, future service as Constock, host body to be determined by assessment of psychological staff, yeah yeah we know that, though," and here he points to the camera, "sloth, sloth is what I recommend, a recommendation that I'm sure will fall on deaf ears, and whereafter his brain and various supporting nervous and sensorial etcetras will be delicately—really, *delicately*?—placed into the corresponding and so on, and so on, of a previously-innocent program-approved beast of the kingdom. Beast of the kingdom, love that phrase."

Gavel comes down.

And Sophi is crying. I put my arm around her, pull her close. "The tart was good," I say. She sobs, saying, "Oh I'm so glad, but why do they have to be innocent, Bones? Can't they find guilty sheep instead? I mean they're so cute, and they'll... kill them... just to..."

"Sheep?" I say.

"Oh, they have a glut of Shetlands," she tells me.

All waiting in line.

# Part Three

## IN SHEEP'S CLOTHING

*A Brief History of Several Failed Escapes*

Somewhere in the dusty recesses of my well-travelled, much-traumatized brain there's a montage and it plays repeatedly, flickers, creaks a little, causes nervousness and an irritable bowel. If my brain were an oyster, then this is the grain of sand that creates such pearly nightmares. Every now and then the montage loops longer as a new alarm is added, a new scene, a new shot of adrenaline to keep the spool spinning, the fool fleeing. Examples?

It was raining. Weasel and I had gone fishing. The boat, stolen, leaked, and so we took turns bailing. Neither of us knew how to fish but we had rods and worms and one paddle to lead us home.

It was raining. I was locked out, had fresh fruit and a baguette. She came to the door with a black eye, shook her head, No.

It was raining. Clouds hung low like torn wool, and if I had less footing, I did have cover. The alarm shrieked like a bird of prey or maybe that was just the blood in my ears, the montage on overdrive. I've been here too many fucking times, I was thinking, as my legs were moving. Just once let the path be clear, let the fence be low, the pursuers fat and clutching clogged arteries. I ran expecting the burning net of the perimeter, expecting wolves to spring out of the soft green turf. I ran a fast straight line down rolling hill after rolling hill, into the mist, into what felt like safety...

Exhausted, we barely made it to shore, the rain became a torrent and Weasel, no longer proud of his tiny fish, started to freak. I can't fucking swim, man. Lightning flashed around us. Three men with three weapons awaited us onshore:

Tire iron, two-by-four, hairnet of golf balls.

Fuck, man, said Weasel...

Her eyes peered over my shoulder as a man came up behind me, threw a heavy, tattooed arm around my neck and lifted me into the house. Aw shit just let him alone, he's a sweet guy. Smack. Thump. An apple rolls down the steps, the baguette is crushed under foot...

There was nothing in me, nothing to keep

me going, I would collapse soon but when I did I could lick the dew from the grass, that would be nice, or I could eat the grass, dammit, I could eat the grass, I could eat the fucking grass there's food all around me. I'm a fucking sheep, I've got four fucking legs and a muzzle. Jesus! Giddiness kicked my legs higher: no one was following, the perimeter was behind me, my brain was well packed and not wobbling loosely—yes, they did a fine job those crazy surgeons. Now how do I slow down? Sheep on overdrive. Might as well run some more. Lift legs and fly, Bones, skim over the rolling green a rocket into the mist, ears back and fleece rippling. Moved into a trot, then, a flying, landing, flying trot and a field awaited, a golden field of crackling oats and sugarcane, in the centre a picnic blanket, checkered red and white, a basket of fluffy buttered bread and apricot jam, ha ha don't eat the basket, Bones, you inbred cousin of a goat! Eat it all and drink the dew and lie down and sleep, sheep, the sun will protect you, the eagles will keep watch, the clouds puff by saying count me I count you and the turf began to level out and... What the hell is that?

Weasel, soaked, stripped off his clothing when we reached shore, said, Hello, gentlemen, your fine boat's a piece of shit, and not the kind that floats, and then turned and ran back into the water, threw his hands into the air and shouted, Strike me dead now, O Lord of lightning. It rained harder...

And somehow, I worked my neck free of his arm, perhaps by pretending I was unconscious, caught him off guard and pushed him against the wall, ran to the far end of the mobile home, to the bedroom where Minka and I had writhed all night. The window was too small to jump out of, so I stood on the bed.

He's got a knife! Minka screamed.

He's got a tire iron? Weasel whined.

The reel spins and grows longer, this is a new thing, this tall black stone, and new things draw curious sheep too close. The new thing might kill, isn't that horrible? Yes, that's horrible so run to it, slow down, slow down, wow that's a tall black stone in the middle of the green, tall and black and slick and awfully phallic, isn't it? Cock of the watch and run away, little sheep, is what it crows.

Sigh. But you can't run anymore, and you can't row anymore, and you had one surprise in you, should've clocked him not shoved him, he's a got a small head but a big body and the way he holds the knife shows he knows.

In the movies she shoots him in the back, right?

They started to follow Weasel into the water, but you could see the confusion, the indecision, as he kept wading deeper. Woohoo, strike me dead you great lizard in the sky. I rowed out to Weasel, tried to pull him into the boat, which didn't want to float, but he hung on to the side, said, Fuck man, I don't know what I'm doing. We drifted like that to the centre of the lake, me bailing, Weasel saying his dick was so small now a minnow could swallow it in one bite.

Then the sun shone, a breeze picked up, and we drifted to the other side, stumbled ashore when we saw an inflatable rubber dinghy racing after us from the other side,

Weasel shouted, You guys got my clothes?

She was screaming, Stop, stop, and the small-headed big-bodied man did stop, in the doorjamb, said, So how many times did you fuck her? and I said, Last night, or this month? He snorted. Sorry, I said, thought she was, you know, available. He pointed the knife at a photo on the wall, happy couple in leather, she on his lap. Said you were her brother, I said. He laughed, said, You're a joker, she likes those, but no one fucks my wife without asking me first. And when they ask me, I mess them up.

That surprises me, I said.

You haven't answered the question, shit for brains.

Three, I think.

He turns, looks back. Was he good?

Jesus, Woody, just let him go.

I didn't like his calm. When bad men are calm bad things happen, which was a quote from Hog. What would Weasel do? Fucking run, man...

Give me your fucking pants, man, said Weasel.

We ran through the forest till we came to water again.

Aw it's a fucking island, Bones!

There's no escape, says the tall black stone, the small-headed man, the island. You've no right to expect escape, because what you're running from is inside you, it's that brain in your skull, it's that montage spinning in your psyche, and you run thinking, aha, finally I've made it, but it's like a staircase by Escher, or a funhouse mirror, and you'll only succeed when you stop running, accept imprisonment, enjoy the scenery, the banter, the pretty girls, the rubber walls.

She's lonely, man—can't you see that?

Is that true, Minka?

Crying behind him. He turned to her and that was the chance I'd been waiting for, threw the duvet over his head and leaped and shoved once again and this time he fell over a lamp table and out I was, grabbing the baguette on the steps and out into the rainy morning, to my car, to find the tires slashed....

We circled along the shore, hid behind the sprawled roots of a fallen fir, watched the three as they argued and tore the rowboat apart. I think we're going to see some bags of white powder, Bones, said Weasel, and yes, they had them, and Weasel grabbed a water-weathered rock, lobbed it grenade-style into the forest, and the three went running after and we sprinted for their inflatable, hopped in and, me at the helm, Weasel at the engine, hollered as we sped away, cried with laughter as we neared shore, shouted curses as the engine sputtered, out of gas, and three more men waiting...

There was an opening in the tall black stone, and inside a spiral stairwell. I climbed to the first landing, rested, climbed to the second landing, rested. Stairwells aren't made for four legs. At the third landing I napped and when I woke the sun was shining through a small, porthole-like window. The floor was littered with pamphlets, I now saw, and the pamphlets had words, yes, words like Welcome and Watch Tower and Constock and pictures of pigs and sheep and cows and boys and girls holding hands.

Five landings later I was at the top.

*Why Not Zombies?*

Mostly, I think he didn't like to work, my shrink. He was more shirk, I think, and at times I questioned his credentials, wondered if there was a six-month course for shrinks, too. Read this, watch this, stare out the window for thirty minutes while I walk away and when I return tell me what you have concluded. Interesting. Not analyzing me at all, going over his grocery list, or his favourite client fantasies. Or distraction, diversion. I'd say, Why does man imprison man? No other species does this. Why does man steal from man? Species don't survive this way. Why are we so fractured, so utterly fucking schizo as a species? And instead of giving contrary references from nature, big monkeys eating tiny monkeys, for example, he'd say, scratching that black and grey beard, You know, Freud hated butter, hated the thought of it spread over things, the mushiness. He called it *smothergrease,* and you realize how significant that is?

"No, I do not."

"Well I will spell it out and you can look at the word."

"What does this have to do with anything?"

"We're a strange, strange species, Bones."

So I'm in his office, he's slid a panel back to reveal a flatscreen and several bottles of scotch, says, "You have to watch this, truly fascinating bit of film making, really have to get the director's name." His cell phone rings and he tells me he has to go pick up his daughter, leaves, locks the door from the outside but not before pointing to the window and saying, "Don't jump," in a questioning way, but we're five floors up and the place is crawling with guards and Constock candidates and the surgery, if it happens (it happens) is still months away and it's surprising how relaxed the mind can be, how time feels infinite when you are submersed in it. Not that people don't panic, and it's all the same, right? It's all survival instinct, don't think about time, don't think about mortality, but do try to survive when threatened. Conflict there. And if my shrink were here, we could avoid talking about it. I would say, It's an over-awareness of time that's the root of all distress, don't you think? Time presses against our will to live, like a shockwave, and instead of fighting it sometimes we....

But he *loved* yogurt, he'd say, throwing it back to zero.

For some reason the film is in black and white. It starts with a Property of CCC advisement, and a 3C Productions credit, and the sound, a drone, a buzzing of flies, then moans, moans of the dead returned to life over a discordant string section. Looks pretty good so far. I pause it and open a bottle of scotch, a Glenmorangie, take a glass from the cabinet and fill it, start the film again. This might be my last film, might as well enjoy it. Educational, he said? Should be planning escape but there'll be time for that later, when desperation sinks in, when the adrenaline flows and all things are possible. You can't fake desperation, just as you can't fake inspiration. The scotch is sparky, I raise the glass and say, "OK, Zombies, here's to you and your mouldy brethren."

The glass is soon empty and another poured.

Why are blood and gore so much more disturbing without colour? So much more primal? How different would the world be, would *we* be, if they messed up our rods and cones and gave us monochrome instead of rose-coloured? Where's my goddamn shirk? He needs to answer this. Zombies in line in a shower room, monosyllabic and eager for soap. Zombies mindlessly rubbing up against each other, some kind of lather lust, Jesus. A third glass and I'm lying on my back watching the ceiling spin while Zombies answer questions about the Bible. It's a game show. What is represented by the Burning Bush? *Granghk, meat*. What is the primary theme of Noah and the Ark? *Granghk, poopoo, hargh hargh*. When Moses comes down from the Molehill, what is he wearing on his feet? Zombie vomits. There is nothing to be learned from Zombies, comes the dramatic voice over.

The bottle is empty.

It has gotten dark and once again the Zombies are rising from the dead, trolleyed out of the mortuary to the CCC for Zombies castle, have their old brains removed, chopped up, replaced by a simple circuit board, are stood up and told to walk. They walk. They mostly avoid walls, they manage not to drown themselves at the cafeteria trough, But after a while where's the fun in this? says the man in white. And where's the punishment?

More scenes of Zombies adjusting to prison life. It's dark and it's all so familiar. Where's my fucking shirk? Ceiling spins and the film starts again, the strings, it's very annoying and when did I move next to the window? Sleepy. Oh god there's puke on the side of my face, great, just great

Bones, this will get you a fine recommendation from Dr. Shirker, wherever the hell he is. Oh, I might get into trouble, fuck. Ha, fuck, trouble? What will they do? Can't stand up, so grunt, fling the bottle at the screen, and all goes quiet and the room tilts and I slip out, flap and land softly in the wet grass, ignore the Zombies walking the grounds, listen, listen to the birds burrowed in the soil and in the zigzag morning I'm thrown into a canvas sack, am dragged to a bed and treated for various cuts and scrapes and broken bones, "Bones, can you hear me?" And I hear the head doctor, his flute voice saying, "It was all part of my study of the criminal's mind, that he went through the window tells me what I need to know." "Can you hear me? Hey?" Woman leaning over me. "Hmm, I know you, you're..." but she puts a finger to my lips and kisses my forehead, "We have someone in here," she says, and, "We haven't forgotten, OK?"

My shrink comes over, says, "You look like shit, Bones," smiles, asks the pretty nurse if she wants to get coffee, and off they go, she looking back, shrugging her shoulders and I call for a real nurse, some painkillers, hair of the dog, anything. When she comes I say, "He spiked it, spiked my drink, then tried to take advantage of me and when I resisted he threw me out the window, the perv," but instead of sympathy, a hand on my forehead, she rolls me into the bright sunlight and says, "It's because of your lies that you are here, scum."

"At the window?

"Water?"

But she's gone. I moan, bring my hands to my aching head and notice the stitches in my arm, slide my hands down and feel the neck brace, look at my legs under the blanket and see where the amputation took place, where another's legs have been grafted, and it's all wrong, they're sideways, I'll walk funny and what's with the dirt all over them? My heart races. "Nurse, nurse, I call," but she's still here, hasn't left, says, "Oh really you want us to give you nice new legs when you'll only need them for what, a week? Aren't we selfish, scum?"

"They're rotted, Zombie legs!"

In the afternoon the blinds are pulled. The sound rouses me. I've been restrained at the wrists and ankles. "Surgery," I hear, and the bed is wheeled down a hallway and into a bright white room and the nurse sees the panic on my face, smirks, says, "Oh, we should let you suffer but it's just to get the glass out of your ass, honey, and some x-rays, a scan of your brain. That was quite a fall and you're a tad smashed. Can you hear me? Can you hear me?"

*The Land that Crime Forgot*

And on the other side, the Constockade. From the top of the watchtower I had a lay of the land, though I had to push the Information desk to the window, and then a chair so that I could jump on the desk, but once up I could see from whence I came. And there were maps, too, and interactive screens, but as a sheep I simply needed to see. As a sheep I needed to know this wasn't a tomb.

The mist had cleared and sun was high. Across the land nothing stirred, no people, no beasts of the field. The concept of days of the week entered my mind, as did the concept of Sunday, and holiday. Or maybe no one cared anymore. A path led from the tower but it wasn't very worn and it led down, over a river, through some trees, snaked out of sight. The city I could see beyond this, sparkling through the haze. And on the other side of the tower the climbing green hillside, inconspicuous except for the dark square of an occasional underground doorway. And a little farther up a line of slim silver poles that must've formed the perimeter. Could I see movement? Wolf guards? And climbing more gently, fields and pastures, and more faintly the barns and coops. A telescope at the window presented a momentary challenge but allowed me to see the distant sheep and cattle, a pen of pigs but no black cape, and a few dogs racing, and every now and then a vehicle and people, and my eye started to water and my brain reject such a narrow view of the world.

And I needed to eat.

I jumped down from the desk. Was there nothing here to eat? These brochures? Maybe a child dropped some candy? Sniffed around but nothing. A bird landed in the window and startled me, though I think it was just as startled and flew off. It was red, a warning, perhaps, or a reminder of Robyn. Thank you, bird, or brain. I had to get to the city and find Robyn, and Wren, and a good lawyer. Yes. And a sympathetic surgeon. I couldn't stay this way. Where was my body? On the Isle of Conquestador? How would I find Robyn? What about the gang? Fuck the gang, says the sheep in the tourist tower, fuck them for fucking you over, Bones, fuck Goose, fuck Hog, fuck Weasel. Should you really have expected anything other than cowardice? But maybe they had no choice. Dude, there is no honour amongst thieves like us. But if you were in the same position,

Bones, if you could save two friends by giving up one, would you? No, no I wouldn't sacrifice the one to save the others, let us all go down together! This ship is our oyster. Surely someone spilled something, some sticky juice residue, or dropped half a sandwich, or gum? A sign said washroom so I went inside, a light flickered to life when I pushed the door open, and here I was trotting to a toilet and about to drink when some sense returned. But all attempts at standing and opening the sink's taps proved comical. Somewhere it's on video. I peered into the toilet. I examine the urinal. Couldn't do it.

Left the washroom.

Tried to ignore the propaganda on the walls, the photos of very repentant looking Constock, the pensive goat staring at the sky, the weary pig in muck, a Shetland pony seeing the innocence of children for the first time. Under each photo, the corresponding human (male) mugshot and history of the criminal, with murder always in red and bold. I wasn't doing a good job ignoring this, was I? I had to get to the city, I had to get my brain to my old body before it was too late, I had to be able to stand to turn on fucking taps, to not always have my ass in the air. Was I here? On the wall? The infamous Bones Alone? I walked the circular room. No Bones. Where was Moll? I wandered and found him, unrepentant, his biography serving as warning. That's one angry pig. Someone had taken a felt marker to Moll's face and scribbled *I'm Hungry* on his forehead, which I was. So fucking hungry and anxious from reading this, this was no place to be and how long till someone came up the stairs? Trash the place, Bones, do it. Do it and run.

Run? I hadn't even the energy needed to leap down the stairs. But I could fall, fall and be done with it all, tumble down the stairwell.

I probably don't roll well.

But see that, Bones, sheep-brained twit? A special door, with a simple button.

No, where is it?

Right eye, Bones.

That square thing?

It's a box that falls.

But that doesn't sound safe.

It is made by Man.

Am I Man?

That is an interesting question.

Before entering the falling box I made sure to take a good shit and place it just so, just exactly so, so that the next tourist, the next fat, ugly, stupid, squat, selfsame upright tongue-wagging sightseer would have his legs fly out from under him, would land on his rippled, tail-less ass, would have his round head bounce twice off the hard floor with an amusing hollow sound and wake, finally wake, with confusion and dull wit and the inability to stand. Who are these people? What is this place? What smells so bad? Aww, look at the pretty little animals.

Nosed the elevator down.

Are you a sheep in sheep's clothing, Bones?

\*

You are the first in so much of what you do, thinks the sheep in the elevator, which has no music, though music is heard. The passenger capacity sign does not mention sheep, does not say eight men, ten women, fifteen sheep, twenty children. The Fall of Man includes no mention of sheep, or none that one can recall. Lambs are another matter. And the sheep came to Eve in the night, its eyes red like fire. And no coat of arms or battle tank is emblazoned of mutton. The sheep in the elevator paces a little, shakes its head back and forth. You and what army? He who made the lion made thee, meekest of meek. And inherit the earth talks only of a plot in soil, don't get it wrong. But you are the first in so much of what you do, thinks the sheep. No one suspects you, thinks the sheep. That is your advantage, thinks the sheep. Before leaving the world you were left a phone number, a business card, under a broken flagstone near your home, so you will get to the city and you will call that number. Yes you will. The sheep shakes its head back and forth. Crazy. The elevator stops, the doors open, the sheep moves down the sunlit path, the black tower vanishes from view. The sheep crosses a footbridge. It's a slow Sunday at the park, the trees offer shade and grazing ground. Stop and stay here, thinks the sheep, who later hides under the bridge from the man who mows the grounds. Under the bridge where catfish trawl and sheep sleep along the riverbank.

### *Broken Bones*

There are seven floors at the CCC, and each one has a different name. I had been wheeled about throughout each of these floors, some containing doctors' offices, others endless dormitories, or operating rooms. On the third floor is the Cattle and Crooks Cafeteria, where the food is of dubious origin, while on the fourth is the Constock Cranium

Cruncher, with computers and doctors and pale green light. The second floor is the Crazy Critters Cooperative, where constant experimentation takes place, I am told, where one day I spy a Rhesus Macaque smoking a cigar. Officially, when you enter the CCC complex, it's the Centre for Criminal Correction but on the top floor it says Centre for Constock Conversion.

I spend three weeks recuperating on the sixth floor, the Centre for Convalescent Cons, after my fall from the fifth floor, the Couching and Coddling Centre, and it does not go by quickly. From time to time I see my shrink, the good doctor, but he's mostly moved on to new patients, is pushing for the inclusion of aquatic mammals in the program, believes we have a fishy past, humans, sticks his arm under a running tap just to show the patterns in the hair. "For swimming apes!" It's while in bed at the CCC that the news comes that once I'm healthy enough to survive the twelve-hour surgery I will be divested of my current bodily form and the thus final stage of the beginning of my sentence. It's anticlimactic. Hey, anything to be able to walk again, I say, but they don't laugh, this white-gowned committee. There will be very little use for humour when you are a sheep, I am told. My shrink phones me and says, "Well even if I had said, no no he isn't fit for the program, no one would have listened." He suggests I cry.

I am asked if I have any requests for visitors while I still can converse. I am told that anyone who requests will also be able to see me after the surgery, a viewing of the new form. But there's no one. No family, and the gang is in prison. And yes, that's a bit sad, but the gang was pretty much all I had and not even Hog's mother, rest her nasty soul— for she did not survive the surgery—not even her surprise visit—she too was at the CCC—cut into the boredom of those last three weeks. They wheeled her in and she sat with a hand on my knee and a twinkle in her left eye. She was paralyzed from the waist down, had gamely taken a handful of bullets defending her dear boy, shrugged it off and surely died on the operating table just to spite the doctors, the government, those who took her son from her, humiliated him in Play Prison, though I made no bones about letting her know that I felt betrayed, ranted, I must admit, while she sat and her dim grin sloped to a frown. "Hog'll be out in what, six months? Yes, six months? Nod if you hear me. Was that a nod? It was, wasn't it? Six months! Six months and the others, too. I've seen the news, Missus Hog,

I've seen it all. Six months for trying cover up my, my, my murderous rages. I heard Goose say *who knows how many he really killed, he hid so much from us*. Hog, he knows better. But what is it? What do you see? He said you were fucked like that, saw things that were coming, said you knew the day he'd get out of jail before he even went to jail, wrote it on an envelope and hid it away, and when he got out you showed it to him. That's a really messed up thing to do, isn't it? What kind of mother are you? So why didn't you warn us? Or did you?"

They wheel her away, they wheel me away, everything wheels when they cut the cord, the one that connects the brain stem and spinal column, girls sit around in pyjamas and play spin the brain, kiss each other and giggle and no one caresses the brain in the middle, wonders who it was, was he handsome, a good lover? Could he make people laugh? And they spin it with sticks, actually, won't touch it. Ew. Gross. There's no cure for terminal boredom. "Bring her back," I shout. "I won't yell at her again, I promise."

I have a fractured fibula that's slow to heal, and a tibia that looks like some geeky kid's failed woodshop jigsaw puzzle, and of my ribs three are broken and one is still missing. I wait, wait, but

Hog's mother's just like the others, really, they see something that pulls them in but then back off quickly. I would have liked a wife, you know, would have liked that quiet morning routine and she wouldn't have had to've been beautiful in any fashion model way, no, I've always preferred plain Janes, just nice skin and a healthy sex drive and she could have saved me. Analyze me. My shrink said, in a rare moment of insight, which I think he had lots of but refused to surrender easily, he said that I needed to stop thinking I'd messed up, stop thinking that if my life skipped again it'd play out differently. You're a wobbly table in a pub, Bones, accept it. There's a piece missing and it will always be missing and no amount of coasters will fix that wobble.

Coast. I've always wanted to coast.

So for the next week I have no visitors. They keep an eye out for internal bleeding, Crush Syndrome (the weight of your sentence, ha ha), bring in interns, an amazing story of survival though Alcohol Flop, but they look my chart over and say, "Hey he's pretty much fucked anyway. Whoa, dude. Murdering is, like, baaad Karma." "I was young once, too," I shout as they leave, then call for a doctor, a lawyer, a friend. Even the fly that'd been keeping me company by landing on my nose every five minutes is gone. In the future they will scatter you, shatter your essence into a thousand shards then prick the flies' brains.

The days at CCC end the same way, with the sun setting outside my window, the light falling and the blinds being pulled right at that moment where the light would have gone green, but you can't see green here, it's too easy on the eyes, it's the colour of hope. One day there's a letter from Sophi saying she's exhausted all avenues, has done everything she can but no one listens to her, they go all blank-eyed when she talks and she's thinking of a new career, though she isn't sure which one, wonders if I think travel and tourism would be a good choice and I find myself thinking it over. She says, as well, that she's sorry she hasn't come and visited me, but hospitals make her faint, knees get rubbery. She thinks about my eyes.

I write her back asking if she can take care of one final request, which concerns my belongings, those that were seized from my room near Froggies, namely the books. I can't just let books rot in a storage bin, grow mold and never be read again. There are some gems, I tell her, read them, pass them along. And there's a great leather jacket, a bit worn but fleece-lined and the warmest thing in winter. Weasel would always say if you die in my arms, man, your last words had better be, Take my jacket. Please don't let Weasel have my jacket. Please send him a letter saying so. I fall asleep and in the morning the letter is gone.

A doctor chuckles when he tells me I'm healing fast.

"Like wings on chickens," he says as he leaves.

I ask for, and surprisingly receive, alcohol and cigarettes. They're delivered by an ageing nurse whose hair is straight and stringy and grey and she never says anything, sits on the edge of the sponge-bath cart, blows smoke out the window, never bathes me. I imagine we go for walks on the CCC grounds—the well-maintained garden out back—and hold hands, point at things but no, never speak. Who was she? Her cigarette's smoke is carried by a draught of evening wind and then the blind is pulled. My shaky hand raises the last sip of sherry, then that too is gone. The cart's wheels squeak. When I try to remember her name, it's not there.

Measurements are taken of my skull. Callipers are placed near my eyes. Two quick little doctors do this. My morning erections are noted and photographed. The man who does this is not handsome. He is round like an egg, walks with a cane, has a balding head but long frizzy black hair falling like dead ferns. His glasses are thick, square. His voice is animated (he talks to himself) and he seems pleasant enough. He's learned he must measure quickly if he wants full size and when he's done he tucks it back under the sheet, gives it a light pat.

"An important article for the *Constock Reporter*," he tells me, tells anyone who comes near. He even says it to the fake plants. Sometimes he sits at the bed, opens his laptop, goes through the numbers, the photographs. Apparently I'm not the only subject of his study. He has graphs, pie charts. He sings to himself.

And that's how those days go.

*The Country Sheep*

I woke from a night of troubled dreams to find myself transformed into a farm animal, woke lying on my back and waving my black little legs before me. I tried to shout for help but the words came out all wrong, like someone was shaking me, hard. Then there came the pitterpatter of feet and the door to my stuffy old room opened and it was my sister, lovely Goosella, in her morning neon spandex. She chewed her gum, sighed disgustedly, closed the door and called for Mom. And then yes it was my mom, Weaselina, in her bathrobe, who rushed over and tickled me, tickled me until I begged her to stop.

And then she slapped me, I recalled, hooves trying to find traction in the soft mud of the riverbank, slipping. Slapped me and I was on my feet, running around the room and then out of the room, hopping onto an oblong candlelit dining room table where strangers with knives sat. They stabbed at me. I woke. Bees droned over the water. Dragonflies skimmed, landed on reeds, hovered in front of my muzzle. I leaped the last bit of the bank, found level ground. Had the dream continued Hog would have appeared as Father, would have taken control of things, or threw that final spear.

Some dreams leave you feeling cheated.

I lay down again.

It's going to be steamy, I thought. Already the garden flowers were beginning to slouch. A day of storms, and not a day for travelling the countryside. So maybe I'll stay here a while yet, could use another day of rest, a few actually, and why are you thinking this is some kind of safe haven? Maybe you're surrounded by wolves? Sitting, I nibbled on this, that, chewing, looking around, chewing. Grasses aren't so bad. After a while you start to notice the subtle changes in flavour, depending on the age of the grass and the type of grass. The flavours are green, green-green, yellow-green, and brown-green. And yellow-brown-green. Give a quick glance for caterpillars, lower head, and pull. Give a quick glance for inchworms, lower head, and pull. *Now the sense of smell and taste, that's what's called a hybrid system, this one involving sheep receptors and human interpreters, and we really can't say what shit will taste like. But this, like everything else, is something you really don't deserve to know, you lousy crook.*

I got to my feet—hooves, I mean—and stretched.

I was too calm, really. As a sheep you have two modes: panic and Zen. And sometimes you panic when you should be Zen, and vice versa. So I was chewing, looking around—nice buzzing bugs, nice distant hillside prison, my I've got dirty legs, is that a flea biting my ass, mmm green-green, geez Goose in spandex—and didn't hear the bus come up behind me, didn't hear it stop, wait patiently, idle, rev. But I did hear the driver tap the window and I turned and thought that's a thing, that, that thing, sure is, big yeah, and then people leaned out the windows and started taking pictures of me and my sheep and I froze, dropped the long grass stem to the asphalt and casually moved out of the way, casually nibbled more grass (which tasted of diesel fumes!), casually slipped down to the riverbank and hid once again under the footbridge.

Those were people. Yes indeed those were people and how do you feel today, Bones? Oh no I feel very sheepy, I feel country sheep not city sheep. Get this man out of me. This is a nice river and bugs make me happy they're so small and have so much energy, they just go go go don't they? They remind me of the fleas biting my ass oh that's so funny I really don't want to wake up but I should, right? Something is knocking on my mind. Someone is walking on the bridge. Bah. Bah bah. "Oh it's down there," I hear them say, no I'm not a sheep sheep can't understand that stuff, that watery hissing and quacking they call language. My oh my they must live in madness, always zooming around like bugs and so stupid why don't they just get on all fours but no they have to stick their heads way up high to hide their bald spots yes. Shame they don't know how funny we are. They don't know because we sheep have no thighs to slap.

And they moved along, and there were promises of many sightings of the prison stock and even a guard wolf had been arranged, so up to the tower, everyone, carry on and you'll find it much cooler in there. The footsteps faded and I climbed the bank once more, found myself in the middle of the parking lot not minding the warmth under me but knowing I likely didn't have much time. And what a struggle it was, the sheep's need for rest and my brain's need for escape and there was a sudden, sharp pain where forebrain met hindbrain, a white flash, so I stood there doing nothing, thoughts in a loop, thoughts looping, lie in shade, run away, lie in shade, run away, till it became lying shady runaway, then lions Hades run this way. But where to go? The sheep was right, you'll be lying in a grave if you go a ways today in this heat but no you'll be dragged back to prison to stay the rest of your days as soon as that wolf hears about the cute little stray in the parking lot. So.

Hmm.

Hiding under the bridge isn't going to fool anyone but yourself, silly sheep. It feels safe but there's surrender in it too, you must realize. No, little sheep, I can hear that tiny voice questioning my authority but, and I know this hurts, you are bred for docility, and can you tell me how docility and surrender are different? Well, in only one way:

the docile never have to surrender because they don't start shit to begin with. But we, you and I, Bluebell-7 (minus brain!) and Bones, we have started shit and now we have to get out of shit. You do understand the concept of shit, right? Don't shrug. Would you eat shit? You're not sure. OK. Would you purposefully roll in it? Probably not. It is good? It's just shit, you say. Grass cheese. Well maybe we should try another approach.

Meanwhile, the sun climbed the sky and tour bus number two in the distance churned up smoke so the parking lot was going to fill with buses and maybe the wolf guard was strutting before the tourists *right now* and sniffing it, sniffing sheep, *that* sheep, the one that made fools of us all, hell maybe it was Top Dog himself, so you need to move, but it's too hot to move and I don't want to move, but hey the bus is in the shade, yes, the windows are down in the bus that's in the shade, and the door's open, too.

When the second bus pulled in and the tourists pulled out, stretched their rubbery limbs and began shuffling toward the bridge, I watched them from the cool bus, from the soft seat I'd chosen at the back, and there I felt much safer. "The tour will last three hours," I heard a guide call out, "and please follow all instructions and do not, I repeat, do not venture or wander from the group… you never know what hoards of hungry baby Moll piglets…"

Laughter.

But he wasn't funny.

Hiss quack quack.

I knew these smells, the empty coffee cups, the deodorant, the neck soap and cheap shampoo. I knew the stale smell of cigarette smoke and the sour one of foot fungus. And bus seats reveal far too much. I moved to the floor at the back of the bus and thought no further, emptied my brain, for I'd found my escape plan, I'd take the bus, and either it would work or it wouldn't work. The bus was big, bigger than the crowd that'd gotten off the bus. So there was room to spare. Lots of room for a sheepy sheep. Until then, one could never get too much sleep.

Maybe Father would make an appearance this time. I'll catch that spear in my teeth, snap it in half. And then.

### *The Shitty Cheap*

He never leaves my head, that shrink, and since

my head is in a sheep's head, three's a crowd. He wonders why I miss Jack, who did little else but betray me, and is puzzled by my affection for Fergus. But, he points out, it's long been known that we secretly love what we choose to call ugly or hideous. And your admiration for Moll—no, don't dispute this—is... all too human. The shrink looks sad, but says obliteration is commendable. So, he's not really puzzled at all. Everything is a game, Bones.

So where am I on the chess board?

Chess. That's an interesting choice.

Well, it ain't Monopoly.

Think about that word, he says, pointing his finger.

One many, I say. As in one too many in my head. I wave the shrink away but he's like a fruit fly and makes random flight changes. Or he's like the wasp before my nose, the yellowjacket that's like a lion with a cricketlamb in its mandibles. Despite the heat the summer is fading, isn't it? Kill everything, says the wasp, we are many, devour the world. Ha, paint yellow and black stripes on fluffy me and watch out everyone, no more mister nice sheep. It's a size thing, must be. The warning colours on a whale are not festive because that would be a parade float. Black works writ large. The Universe.

But I think I know, says the bearded fly, why you feel so little fear.

But you aren't going to tell me, are you?

He spreads his spindly arms: Where would the fun be in that?

Well, I don't think I'm a pawn, you know.

That would be too easy, but you probably are.

As in who wants to see themselves as a pawn?

Something like that, Bones.

So my lack of fear must have to do with denial?

You tell me.

I'm telling myself.

He laughs, Yes, we're all in this together.

We've made other nations uneasy, maybe they'll invade us, maybe the head of Constock Operations will be tried by a world tribunal, called a mad butcher, hung and found to have serious micropenis. And our fine Prime Minister, who rules through laughter, through slaughter, through the nation's Yoke of the Day, they'll lock him up and feed him prisonmeat, check his brain for parasites and when, dammit, none appear they'll surgically implant some. Don't worry, just a few brainless worms, won't take up any space at all. Oh no, but look what you've done, smeared your poopoo all over the wall, is that any way for a world leader to act?

The shrink has no inkling of this, does he? He's too in love with his own hamster wheel, shrunk shrink on a roll, ha, furry and determined to get to the goddamned top but falls exhausted, spinning, spinning, flung. Saw the porn hidden there, too, with the glens, in his office, before my tumble from the fifth, saw the ladies with grafted animal genitalia and the doggerel written between the margins, crease poems and smudges of fingerprints, flecks of spittle. There are rare oils in the brain, Bones, and they are distilled by deep critical thinking or horrendous imagery, and when they build up you've no choice but to feed them, these distilled oils. That's all this is. You say, why not make paint with them and that's a great question, but we're not ready for those images, not ready for our nightmares to be inflated like pufferfish (blow his cheeks out). Life began in an oily little pond, you know? And you know...

Voices return, others fade. A boy isn't happy and says, "This sucked ass, Dad," and Dad mutters in agreement. Outside the bus, they are. Or were. For the bus is along the shore of a red ocean where seafoam has gathered, a blood-pink foam billowing around the bus, a singing foam. The moon hangs huge and molten but there is nothing here, just the wind, and the foam, and the bus that shakes in wind and makes a sheep's legs tremble and twitch. Was that Jack barking? Jack saying come, come? No, that wasn't so clever, the wasp says, though whether to herself or to her prey, one can't be sure. Give it up, I wanted to say, let it go and fly. And then the image shifted from wasp to shoes, the bus shook and clamoured as the people clambered aboard and shuffled to their seats, feet I saw, the running shoes, the flip flops and sandals, the elderly slow and the children quick. I tucked my legs in. The wasp dragged the cricket toward some unknown destination, either a nest or the bottom of a shoe. The children came to the back nearer my sleeping sheep to thee but one by one sat, swung their tanned legs, dropped their packages on the floor (a toy prison animal, a colouring guide to Constock). They'd be napping soon. I pulled my legs in further, curled so no one would see me, the sheep at the very back, the waking sheep watching the feet, the struggling wasp, the one boy (blue sneakers) hesitating, moving closer, hesitating, turning around when called, "Jay, Jay we're up here." "But I want to sit," shadow of a pointing arm...

Well, here's the plan, Bones. You'll climb atop the seat, you'll lean back, sit all person-like, and you'll find a coat, yes, a trenchcoat, sure, and you'll slip that on, and a hat, and dark shades, and some jeans, OK, jeans, those fit well now... stick the ends of the jeans in some shoes, sit like this unmoving till you return to the city, or no, no just long enough to fool the boy, Jay, who hasn't stopped talking and asking about your funny face, who has whispered, *Are you a terrorist?* and hasn't caught your inner response about fighting the war on error, yes, that's what you'll need to do, Bones, and when the bus slows you'll distract the boy, or push him over, yes, and you'll leap out the window though a good little terrorist would hold a blade to the bus driver's pale throat, force him to drive to... the city... B-b-but that's where we're going anyway, Bahammed... Shut up, to the flagstone, the flagstone, infidel!

The boy ran the final length of the bus, leaped into the back seat, caused the wasp to drop its songless prey and fly low, low under the seats then up and over and out the door as the last tourists ventured in, no one mentioning the menacing wolf guard they saw, no one saying much at all about the tour, talking only about the heat, the oppressive heat that isn't right, it's too late in the year and the door closing and the boy sitting squarely then turning his head suddenly and not pausing at all before shouting, "Hey, there's a dog..." and stopping then, because no, that wasn't a dog at all, it was a, a, a sheep, a sheep that was looking right at him, a sheep that had raised its sheep paw thing to its mouth and while shaking its head back and forth was softly hissing and so the boy, Jay, he leaned in and did the same, seemed the best thing to do, really, reassure the sheep, who looked a bit worried, move over and pet the nice sheep on the head as the bus rolled out of the parking lot.

### *A FakeBrain™ Adventure (and Bones A-bed)*

That morning they both woke with shaved heads. Both sat up and, one in a tiki hut on the Isle of Conquestador, the other in a sterile hospital bed, turned to the sun. To one the sun was a yellow frog on a windowpane, to the other the sun was a distant, cyclopic god that coldly glared back.

The sun-frog sucker-gripped the sky and began a slow climb. Feet which were soil grippers like the tiki hut and shuffled toward the water.

While he slept, had they mapped out his skull, measured the phrenological terrain and concluded he was inveterate chattel, or had they seen a skein of back roads that led to nowhere but swampland? The stubble felt odd. The mirror said *lice*? Funny, but the brain said little.

There are no more doctors to measure the depth of your nasal passages, to caress the occipital and parietal and ooh and ahh over it all. This is the morning the one-eyed sun god will blink and all will go black, Bones. Pull the blinds now. Go back to sleep. You have minutes, minutes, don't waste them.

Meanwhile, clop clop went the island feet, and he could not *not* look at them. But did he really need them? Broken wing things, they were. For months you were suspended, swaying in the tectonic lurch of the land, and they came and they went and the electrodes—you know that word well—kissed your NeoPlastic skin, imbued your world with impulses of light that were wisdom. A shuffle, a gait. A fist. The first exoskeletal adventure and they called you Gimpy. The name stuck.

Ah, childhood.

And in the hallway their hearts raced, the men and women in the white coats in the Centre for Crazy Creeps, and they discussed the calmness of the patient, hands over their mouths saying, "But we are about to, essentially, kill the thing," and a white coat thought of that first foetal pig, the sweet scent of formaldehyde, the ham sandwiches his mother made every lunchtime, and of his need to cut into things, and how if he stopped he'd surely slice something off himself, but tall she was now saying, "Studies have been done and" shrug, shrug, "look it up, the brain cannot exist in a panic mode for long, minds have been bred for stability," sure, but by whom? And they looked around then, stopped, pushed against the wall and went back from whence they came, went over the procedure while the patient nee Bones lay on his side wondering if he should run into the washroom and masturbate one last time, the shame of being caught still too strong and he wasn't exactly aroused, but the other, the sand clopper, was, but didn't give it much heed, it wouldn't help him fly.

Eventually he came to a beach. But that wasn't right. He turned his back to the beach and waited and when he turned around again it was gone, and so was the light, but that was a distraction anyway. Cradle. Swoon. Temperate. Anodyne. Stereo. Compulsion. Ova. If the water was wrong then he had to climb, and the best mode wasn't the cartwheel, nor the crab crawl, it was the wingless soil gripping clop. Job. No: jog. It was no body's job to jog and this one wasn't made for it, that he knew, but it felt more like flying than standing and a metaphor said the heart was an anchor dragged along the mud, dredging up shellfish and nucleic chains. They gave you eyes on the ninth day, Gimpy, gave you ears on the twentieth, left the television on all night and eventually you understood that the only important thing was movement, that when movement was gone you were sad. Did you understand the Joke? Do you think he watched? Monitor shows he did. Gimpy, hello?

There was a part of the brain, Bones knew, that could slow things, slow like the forbidden sun this morning. For a few seconds he wanted to stretch minutes into eternity, wanted to fall into a side story, branch off into a new life, a life lived fully, a wife and children and music and friends at his deathbed, sad-eyed but smiling, his last breath, tears, but all which came to mind and eventually brought him to his feet was a story of a hanged man's fantasy of escape as he dropped, neck snapping like a dry twig. The sun rose over the leafless horizon.

Think yourself into a new existence, Bones.

The body, he knew, for he had listened, for he had ears then, ears that understood before they knew he understood, the body, this body, this flightless dodo, this jumbled turkey leg, had a name, too. Jawndoh, which meant found by the

River Comatose. Comatose flowed gently, he knew. Comatose was the world river, but was a horse on the land. A syringe, she said, contains no fewer than fifteen thousand initiations, isn't that amazing? Each initiation contains another fifteen thousand possible initiations. And in that way, my dear Gimpy, you will learn...

He was in his drab tunic, knees shaking, standing at the door. He could hear them out there, talking about him. Cutting him. Let's find someone else, he thought, run out and no, wait for a nurse, anyone, strangle then hide in the bed and take his or her clothes and run, run so fast the guards won't see you. He peeked. Four of them in the hallway, three men and one woman and she was a tall one, long legs, a sprinter. He knew her voice. Her whisper. One looked his way and he shut the door, slipped back into his bed. Maybe this would work out after all? That was what the brain needed to believe, the brain didn't like this drama and told the heart to calm down, told itself, You're only panicking because you think you should panic, but in fact you are calm, and curious. It'll be fun to be a sheep, Bones. You can lie in the grass and sleep all day. And anyway, you never deserved more than that.

Insults, always.

Down the CCC hall a cart's wheels squeak.

And you dreamed of a body, they told you of a body, you saw their bodies with your newfangled apparatus, your EyePod, and you liked their bodies, for they were young and fit but Jawndoh was pale, bruised easily, it was a suit of flabby flesh that flapped but never flew. Clop, clop along the shore, the slick sun climbing, falling back down into the world river, the ocean, the Pacific, sizzling then croaking back to life, four bulbous tipped fingers reaching above the horizon and gripping, clop, clop. Fences. Doors. Locks. The syringe pierces the FakeBrain, yes you know what it is, yes that was one initiation too many. The syringe pierces like a tooth into an apple the day she says with breath, We really have no idea what we're doing, Gimpy. And sorry, no exoskeletal frolic today, we're all out of lube, baby...

The door opens, a voice calls out "Good morning, rise and shine" and the curtains are thrown open, the gurney is polished, and do they wear wings to bring you luck on your day of metamorphosis, the day their magic spell turns your brain into an ass, the witches? No, those aren't wings, when you turn you see they're wigs. The panic is real now. Arms grab hold of you as you sing your catatone, as they lift your useless body onto the gurney, shackle you down so you don't flap wildly, don't spill the cart full of apples to where the horses run free, it's a long plane plain and then what? There is no fence here. Clop, clop you do your jog job, sensors saying you're hot as a frog now, wires sizzling within mesosynthetic head-meat, but there's nothing ahead, no fence, no sea, only sky, for this is the south side of Conquestador, where all the topless robots drop, where the uplift cliffside falls forever, where your feet, your feet, your feet...

The gurney lurched then.

## Rock it, Robyn

*Any world that ends in chaos mimics its beginning*, says the nurse pushing the gurney much too quickly. "There's poetry in that, Bones," she says. Her long strides have left the others behind; I see them receding down the hall, a bit confused, looking at each other and only now running, shouting. "This place is like a fortress," I say, sitting up a little and holding onto the sides before Robyn reaches forward and forces me back down. We take a corner sharply and soon another is running alongside and we race past stunned onlookers, Robyn shouting, "Out of the way, he's bleeding from his spine," and the other, Wren, apparently a former high school football star, stiff arms the boldest of staff, sends them flying and left, right, left we go, Robyn skidding around corners, the gurney shuddering. "We've got people on every floor," she tells me, "people controlling the entrances and exits! We can't fail, Bones, because there's no room for failure here, just do your part and hang on."

Behind Robyn I see Wren, stopping, pulling out a gun, no, wait, a Super Soaker, and spraying the followers with something so thoroughly disgusting they immediately stop, drop, and gag. What the hell is that? "We've got six more floors," Robyn says when Wren catches up, "and you've only got three Soakers in your backpack, go easy on them." Wren nods. Whoa, when did Wren become subservient?

"Fucking chaos," Robyn smiles. "I love it."

The first elevator is open, waiting. We slam in. A short man of middle eastern descent is on his cell phone, nods at Robyn and Wren and says, "We're still holding them, all of them." The elevator drops. Robyn is sweating and breathing hard and Wren wipes her brow. They kiss passionately. The little guy turns his back to them and looks me over while Robyn's hand steadies itself on my knee. Fifth floor... fourth floor... "So, you're the dude, huh?" He looks at my skull, smiles, says, "They've drawn little sheep on it. Funny."

Robyn, red chested, pulls herself away from Wren, says, "Bones, Bones, we have it all planned out. You will be our spokesperson, yours will be the face of our movement... Well yours and the poor little sheep we're also rescuing right now. We have our special ops in the CCC barn, they've been sleeping there for days, disguised as sheep. My idea. We'll save him and he'll be our mascot. We'll put an end to this." Wren's hand is on her ass.

The third floor passes, then the second floor. Wren raises the Super Soaker to his shoulder. A yellow-brown liquid sloshes and I ask what it is. "Fox piss and lube, stinky and slick," says Wren without humour. "My idea," whispers Robyn. And Robyn, I want to say, when we get out of this will you teach me how to be you? And will you do it in bed with those legs wrapping me in a vice, and can we send the video to my ex-gang, and to the judge and my several incompetent ex-lawyers? Hell, let's even show it to sheep. How have you done this so quickly?

The little guy says, "Shit, we lost the parking garage, repeat we no longer have control of the underground," and just then Robyn punches the button for the CCC lobby, grabs one of the Super Soakers and throws it to me, asks if I know how to use it and after catching it with my face and undoing the wrist restraints the elevator reaches bottom, Wren slaps the close-doors button, the elevator rises, dings, and the doors flash open. "VIVA PETABBY" Robyn shouts and I decide to lie on my side and spray the floor, hoping Wren will take them out at the eyes, and it's chaos, alright, blue-suited security grappling with PETABBY infiltrates, two of which are dressed like sheep. Wren and I provide cover while the little guy and Robyn push toward the stairwell, because the bus is down there, and we have to free our own down there, and we have to get the sacrificial sheep to safety, for the sheep is already in the bus and Wren reaches for the final Soaker, Robyn's legs are Olympic, we fly to the stairwell, the doors crash open and "Fuck," I'm screaming, "fuck fuck fucking stop!"

But it's a too late.

And afterwards, but only afterwards, do I realize that of course I could have gotten up out of my rolling bed and at the very least stumbled quickly down the stairs if someone had just stopped for a second, but all this was impromptu, unplanned, and poorly executed. See, the little guy, his back to the stairwell, tries to grab the gurney and lift to carry his end but Robyn thinks his legs can take bigger strides than that, and you know where this is going, and of course it's all going downhill, downstairs, and that's our downfall. The gurney pitches forward, Bones (that's me) flies into the wall, Robyn tumbles with the gurney, Wren tumbles over Robyn and the little guy is beneath all of that.

And everywhere, slick fox piss.

Then Wren grabs Robyn, drags her away, down the stairs to the basement, she kicks her feet, is bleeding from her angry desperate activist face and it's the last thing I see before blacking out. Nice try guys, really, that was one hell of a plan and it would have worked out had you held the basement, in theory anyways, and I'm glad you made it to the bus, broke through the barriers, eluded the police and returned to obscurity, and too bad you got the wrong sheep, but they really do all look alike, shame about that, but you don't seem to have clued in to this crummy universe of mine, where I'm the dog that trusts everyone, I see you and I jump for joy, you show me a bone and say, Good doggy, do you want the bone? and I jump and wag and bark and you throw the bone and I run, run not because I want that bone so badly but because I want you to see how good a doggy I am, how obedient, how faithful. So I run fast until I'm at the sudden end of my leash—oh that's funny, so funny, got me again, you sure did, works every time, and now, yes, laugh, everybody laugh as I slink back into my dog house, neck smarting, pride bruised, but hoping next time, next time you'll undo the leash. Yes, next time. Next time for certain. I'll get that bone.

*Mass Transit, Mass Hysterics*

Jay, it turned out, had a tablet. He started by showing me pictures, funny pictures of bad people in unfortunate situations (a thief stuck in a chimney), then short videos of unfortunate people rising up (old man beating a mugger), and I figured I'd found a sympathetic soul in Jay. Yes, I realized I'd been wrong before—with the gang, with Moll the Pig, with Two Bark—but what's more innocent than a child? Sure, he enjoyed seeing suffering, but there was a morality to it.

I couldn't bleat my approval, couldn't stomp my hooves on the bus floor or even fart, which is the closest thing to laughter for some sheep. At one image of the Prime Minister in a pink diaper I did let out a honk-like sound, which made Jay laugh, which made his father call down the length of the bus and ask Jay what he was doing, at which Jay raised the tablet and nothing more came of it. So I moved my head a little, indicating *next image, please*. And Jay would point repeatedly at an image or video that he found funnier than the others, then hold his belly and pretend to laugh. I'd close my eyes and shake my head. He loved this.

We went through the security checkpoint without problems, left the Constockade grounds, hit the highway into town and all the while Jay and I formed our bond. Eventually he cycled through all the images he had stored except one, which he was reluctant to show me. He peered over the seats. He held the tablet away from me then flashed it quickly to reveal an unattractive nude *person* with the largest and saggiest ass I'd ever seen. Jay seemed to find the image alluring, disgusting, and hilarious in equal measures. I was, I admit, taken aback.

Jay pecked at the tablet's slide-out keyboard, turned the tablet to me.

*Do u know english sheep?*

So, do you mean, do I speak it, or do you want me to pass a message along to Bernie in Liverpool?

I nodded.

*Awsum I knever spoked with a sheep bee4.*

Again, I nodded.

Jay thought, then typed out *do u have aname* then set the tablet on the floor.

This wasn't going to be easy. I raised a hoof and intended to type out, *It's a secret* but hit the wrong keys and hit enter instead of backspace and then *ursa* was on the screen.

*Hi ursa its knice to meat, u.*

My next attempts produced nothing Jay could make sense of. I really didn't have the hoof and tap technique down and it still kind of hurt my brain to make words into symbols. And not to make more excuses but the road was a little uneven. "It's OK," Jay whispered. "I only just learnt to write and I'm a person and we're smarter than sheep." He pet my head.

"Jay," his father called, "why don't you come up here and join us." Jay said he liked it back here but could he have a snack? He winked at me, ran up the aisle but left the tablet, which gave me a bit of time to practice, during which I tried placing a popsicle stick in the cleft of my hoof (no grip), between my teeth (blind spot, couldn't see it!), tried using my nose, my tongue, my strange little elbow and the power of my mind. The last one worked as well as the others. So how the hell was I supposed to turn a key, or use a phone when I got into the city? And how was I supposed to be inconspicuous? And why hadn't I thought about any of this in advance? It'll work out, it'll work out, that's what the voice in my head has always preached and why the hell do I still have faith in it? Because I'm alive? Look at me! This really hasn't worked out. This could not have worked out any more imperfectly. Get up and run. Where? The bus driver, distracted by a distraught sheep—and who wouldn't be?—drove the bus off the road and into the lake.

Jay returned with pretzel sticks. We crunched away. This is good twig, I could have said. Just the right amount of salt. Wonderfully firm. And then I was overtaken with genius more sheep than man, because having hands sets you off ass over head down the wrong track. I typed *yumm* and then *bnose* and nudged a pretzel and flared a nostril and Jay pointed to my nose and I nodded and Jay with the concentration of a surgeon delicately placed a pretzel in my left nostril. I could see it! And in this way I pecked at letters and Jay pressed them for me.

*need help jay.*
*areU a haert sheap?*

Am I a heart shape…

*i am neither heart shaped nor a herd sheep nor a hurt sheep but i need help. i am a scientist sheep. do you know what that means.*

*Lol ulook funnee witha predsalt in yR knose.*

Jay was holding his belly.

*the crazy men at the prison zoo weren't nice to me jay they kept me in a small dirty cage and i want to see my family in the city.*

*Yuk a poopi cage. Do u want2 5end them eemal?my dadhas a phone to.o.*

Well, what *was* my plan? Send Robyn an email? Get in touch with the gang? No guys, the surgery never happened, it's all just ruse by the government. Actually what they do is, get this: they let us go, give us new identities, colour contact lenses, a toupee, a few bucks—they're getting rich off it. All those Constock funds, syphoned off. I'd have to type this of course. Or have someone say it. Jay? Yeah, and they made me look really young, like a boy.

*Wann a hid, in my room ursa?*

I've seen that one before, Jay.

The bus had internet, so I connected, thought a moment, searched for Harvey McLepus, found an entry right away, the murder story, me (terrible photo, see Constock Sentences), and aha, a recent footnote relating to the gang, clicked on that (and by click I mean double pretzel stick tap) and read about the gang's recent release from Play Prison, watched video of Weasel being interviewed, and Hog, too, and where were they? Froggies? Nothing changes.

PETER HOGG (holding back tears): That arseheart cost me my mom...

JERZY WIESEL: I'll miss the game, but not the crime, man. Buy me a drink?

GUSTAV SCHMIDT (middle finger, waves camera away)

And who's the other guy, the blond guy with the muscles and Hog's arm around him like he used to do with me. They met in Play Prison! I stood— they'd replaced me already. They weren't out looking for me, weren't crying into their beers, weren't holding rallies in front of Parliament demanding change, weren't firebombing courts of law. They were drinking. Which, yes, was exactly what I thought they'd be doing but for once couldn't they just surprise me? I stomped a hoof and the tablet bounced. I raised a hoof again and brought it down but Jay snatched the tablet away and handed it to his father who lifted Jay and called for the bus to stop.

"His name is Ursa," said Jay. "And he's a scientist sheep."

"Why does it have a pretzel up its nose?"

"Because he's funny! He told me dirty jokes, Dad."

I made a sheep sound.

Commotion on the bus. Everyone had to get up and see the sheep. "A sheep? Really?" "Oh, just a sheep, sheep are boring," laughter...

"Ursa's a woman's name," said Jay's mother, shaking her head.

"Give him the tablet and he'll tell you," said Jay.

I exhaled and the pretzel flew, then leaped up on the seat and checked where I was. We'd pulled over next to a field, farmland. Could I kick the window out? The bus driver called from up front, saying he had let the authorities know. "They're going to check their inventory. If not, she's all ours." Laughter.

Emergency exit, pull and push out. Hmm...

"Can't we just drop her off? Like, tie her to that tree with a note?"

"With the men in this area?"

More laughter.

Then: "Oh, definitely is a male sheep. Ram, is that right?"

"Bull sheep? What's the opposite of Ewe? Me?"

"Me sheep!"

I jumped off the seat and someone shouted, "Watch it, could be a psychopath!"

"Hey, didn't you mug me once? That was such a *baaaad* day."

So I made cute little sheep sounds, chewed on the upholstery, acted frightened by a leather purse, sniffed Jay's tablet when it was offered, tried to bite it, moved down the aisle closer to the door. Was pet. Bah, bah, bah. Endured lines like, "Hey, Baba, got wool?" And, "When he goes by, don't count him, you'll pass out." And, "Well we can say we got our sheep thrills today." No one cared how funny it was, they all laughed. This is a human sickness, laughter. Mutated crying is what it is. What would my shrink say? Sheep don't cry, Bones, sheep can endure pain, and no one really wants to see a criminal crying. Ergo. I moved farther down the aisle, Jay following me. "Ursa? Ursa?"

Took a bite of an apple offered by a girl, ate potato chips (spicy!) out of the hand of another, didn't have a plan but was hoping one would pop up. I was feeling too dignified to take a crap, which would have gotten me off the bus in a hurry, and I'd eaten so little there was nothing in me. The bus driver? What was he like? Short, pudgy, sitting but holding a fire extinguisher as if expecting me to breathe flames. "We had a goat get in once," he said, "a real charmer. Turned out he was an old guy who'd bludgeoned three wives to death."

The bus went quiet.

I lay down near the door, waited.

When thirty minutes had passed and still no one from the Constockade appeared, and the day had only gotten hotter and the passengers crabbier, knives for eyes, the bus driver leashed me to one of the seats with his belt and got us back on the highway.

Jay defied his father, sat with me.


*Bones' Final Spinal Tap Dance*

From here on in it's foggy. Faces blur and change and it's a doctor I don't know, but then the egg man with fern hair and his frog voice, and then it's my shrink shaking his head, desert wind whistling through the gap in his teeth, and then Wren, hands on head, bereft but no, no that's Weasel looking down saying Jeezus, Bones, as Hog shoves him aside, flashes a light in my eyes and shouts something about emergency sugary, we can't lose this one and why is

Goose holding a needle, I really don't like needles, but Robyn, her skin Nubian black now, hovers over me, buzzes words of solace, smiles and then leaves hand in hand with Hog's mother, out the window, the same window at the end of the white hallway that I'm brought to, the sea is below, breathing apparatus is placed over my mouth and I'm told to count, count while they slide me off the stretcher to my watery grave.

On the sea floor, they pick my bones and whisper.

Harold, Harold, what are you doing down here? That voice. It's my mother, in a clam shell, her body boneless pale, contorted, but her face not aged and she says she likes it this way, this is the True Form, she says, the Divine Bivalve has come for us and it's not too late, Harold, my son, my beloved, join us now.

But the doctor turns, raises a scalpel and my mother jets off.

Jeezus, says sterile Weasel. He's not out. They hold my head under, count to twenty to make sure the baptism takes hold this time, make sure that the soul is free of its kicking fibrous mesh, godammit, that the transfer, the transubstantiation of plain homo to rara ovis aries is without defect and that, brain in hand, held high to the light, severed of its writhing spinal whip, it will shine like a mollusk on stage awaiting its final performance. The theatre is bright and the wet clapping of polypy palms, dance now, dance and speak, fevered brain, dance and squeak and hug the palms along the shore, you phoney, and sing the psalms till the spasms of plasm are no more and all is dark, the clapping subsides, the theatre's walls contract and you hear everything shrinking, the suck of wet and the soft sigh of breathing apparatus. Ah, it's all, that sound now, the rushing in, the rushing out, systolic, Universal, the opening of a fist, a fistula between two hearts beating far below the surface of susurrus, of surcease.

Foggy, I tell you.

*Your mind will be electric, like an eel, you lousy crook. Your mind now is a V4, but when they prepare you for surgery it will be a V8, supercharged. Isn't that nice? See, we experimented with this, did it to ourselves, and wasn't that a blast? In fact, everything we know about how to make you (aka Lousy Crook) into this (insert photo of Bambi) was learned during our own electric daze. But we digress! But do you care? Come on, there has to be something to look forward to!*

*In fact, your jolly little brain will stay in this state for the rest of your much-shortened lifespan. And it has to, to counteract the contraction! Because, dear criminal (i.e. murderer, molester, thug, creep, rapist), we need you to remember how much of a failure you've been, and how much you are costing the state. Some even think (yeah, we're a little loopy from the drugs, too) that there's a place where guilt resides, a negative energy source that we can use to power our dark factories at night, but who has time to get into spooky metaphysics, huh? Not you!*

*You, you, you. It's all about you. It's everywhere, the you. Do you feel dizzy? Why don't you turn the page then? What? This is the last page? But no, look again! Where did that come from? Oh, it's freaky, isn't it? Come on, admit it. OK, we'll come clean. We do love our drugs and like a slug through mud we've brought you down with us, laced these pages with funky chemical essences, Bones—whoa, we even know your name, your fake name, you stupid jerk. We mean, why did you waste it all? You had a good head on your shoulders, you were such a bright boy, you were such a kind boy. What? Muttering something about upbringing? OK, we'll give you a little leeway there, but not much. We've all had it hard. You say, well... Father never praised me, Mother was cold, Brother was a bully. Yeah yeah yeah. So what about us? We've all had it hard.*

*We are sighing.*

*It is too late.*

*The room is spinning and you should be collapsing right... about... now.*

There's nothing else, no memory of vertigo, and why should there be? The inner ear wasn't preserved. There's no feeling of great disembodiment, no feeling of hands on my flesh. There are no preserved images, even though the pamphlet had warned me that it was possible, for the eyes still see. Maybe, when I dream, I recall it all, but the brain has a way of hiding the worst news, and worst news would be the brain seeing itself hovering in the air, dropped into a solution to keep it moist and electrochemical, then once again lifted and positioned, the animal's limbs trembling in anticipation, the surgeons wiping the saliva from their muzzles.

I had of course thought about it. Lying in bed at the CCC. The days getting shorter. They'll wheel me away and I'll panic. I'll scream. I'll fight. Or will I? So how it happened, finding me unconscious in the stairwell, my back or neck probably fractured, it was perhaps the best way. If there's something there, and if it's not just a memory fragment I've inserted on my own, it's a memory of not being able to move, to feel my feet...

After that, it's like trying to remember being

born, or being in the womb. Is there a moment when you are able to remember for the first time? Is it a spark that starts a fire or is it an ember that very slowly grows warmer? What was it about a fence that brought me back? A fallen little fence that any sheep could leap over. And a rooster annoying the fuck out of me. Tinder and spark? Was the fence symbolic? The shrink had said that, yes, had said eventually things will be keys to your memories and you will be back. One former client was brought back by watching a duck love a cat. Who knows what triggers this. Right, and he said he was envious of me, that I had the chance to do this, and I'd offered to trade places and he didn't laugh, just nodded his round head, steepled his hands in front his mouth, and nodded his round head.

Creep.


*Barnstorming*

Once again I was running, running faster than the others and with not much of a head start. And on tired little legs. They spilled out of the bus, through the door, through the emergency exit I'd so perfectly released and kicked open, demanding their money back, demanding their right to more laughter, but soon demanding oxygen and more comfortable shoes. Take them off, run through the grassy field with me, fatties! Ha! Only Jay was able to stay close, and his legs weren't much longer than mine.

You're a pal, Jay, I bleated through clenched teeth while doing a little sheep hop, spinning and turning to face him as he stopped running a few hundred feet beyond the roadside. "Bye, Ursa, I hope you find your family! Send me a email!" I turned, wiggled my tail, made him laugh, then ran toward a nearby copse of trees and stopped in the shade. I needed water. How long till more were after me?

I lay down and watched the roadside, the tourists on their knees, clutching their chests or helping each other up. The bus driver had staggered a little farther than the others, fire extinguisher raised in anger, for it was his wallet I had in my mouth. Really clever of me. Oh I'm a sly one.

I dropped the wallet, nibbled grass (juicy tender shoots in the shade), regained some strength, listened to the birds, remembered a girl who let me see her small breasts and caress her tanned thighs in a copse like this, not far from the road where we'd left our bicycles, when I was young, before I was a sheep.

Before I'd grown old. Before nails were hammered into my muttonized coffin. They'd send someone, certainly. I'll be on the news, no doubt. Some had been taking photos, making movies, some had even run after me holding their phonecams high.

Sigh.

I lowered my head, let the purse slip to the ground, placed the wallet in the purse and nosed the strap around my neck again. Had looked for a white purse, any purse not black, to be less conspicuous, but really it wasn't a purse that was going to give me away. I had money now, though, and credit cards, and a phone, and a compact, chewing gum, antacid, hair ties, panty liners, brushes, gift cards. The jerky video will show a sheep on a bus acting all cute, making those sheep sounds and (laughter) apparently chewing on a purse strap, fighting with it and suddenly the strap is around its neck—it acts panicked, everyone laughs—runs up and down the aisle and then the driver finally relaxes saying what are you a queer sheep you need a big thick black wallet—and holds his wallet out and sneaky sheep snaps it in its teeth and before anyone can get suspicious is up on a seat and kicking out the (already unlatched!) emergency exit and is gone. And although it cannot be proven that the sheep is in fact Constock, a "switcher," we must be wary. Lock your doors, close your windows, a terror may be loose upon our land.

Undid the belt with its teeth! Oh, it was clever.

I left the copse and crossed the field, leaped a wire fence and crossed another field, the sound of traffic diminishing, the whine of sirens fading, trotted through a fragrant cow pasture and then high hay, leaped another wire fence and was in a cornfield, watched for freaky helicopters, listened for hounds on my trail, stayed low in the shade as I weaved through the stalks and pulled up short at a scarecrow then kept moving on and the corn gave way to a little rutted road which I followed before darting back into the corn when I heard a tractor, watched the farmer go by and cut through more corn wondering if they were following me by satellite, zooming in seeing the cornstalks part, graphics showing a green glowing human brain, IQ 137, the red crosshairs staying on my back but clouds, dammit, clouds moving in so they switch to the drone, the angle lower, the drone turning and turning but what's with the signal cutting out? What's with the darkening, cooling skies and what's that rumble?

The first flash, the first crack of thunder startled

me. A second flash followed closely and both man brain and sheep brain agreed: find cover. Sheep brain said tree, but man brain said bunker. Deep, dark. And furthermore, said the man brain, this is the storm that will break the heat, and this sudden grey and this rushing cold breeze and low roar means hurry, means run on all fours because hail hurts and sheep have no hands to clutch at things when the winds swirl, when cows and drones are thrown about like paper toys. But leap a little and see what's ahead. Run and leap, for the rush grows closer and another sound, raucous hammering of metal and thuds all around and...

So sheep know where lightning will strike?

Crashing over there.

The thunder was in my ears and marble-size hail had begun pelting my hide and my head, and the wind swung the cornstalks low. I was confused, circling, trying to keep control of the situation but that wasn't working, so I shut off, sheep knows best, lowered my head and rammed through the last of the corn, leaped a gully and followed what I'd been hearing but not registering, the sound of commotion, the sound of cattle, the sound of sheep. Sure one lightning strike to the barn, sure one little tornado, and this would be a bad decision but the hail was hurting now, hitting like fists, and listen to me, bleating, calling to my kind who were calling back, where's the door, where's the fucking door, in here, in here be safe, come in here, yes but where's the fucking dooooor?

I was in mud, glorious mud, because mud led to the fucking door.

And I could hardly hear a thing once in the barn, for hail was hammering the sheet-metal roof, and the cows weren't happy, and the sheep, all five of them, couldn't shut up either, for the wolf god was angry and there would need to be a sacrifice. Any volunteers? Hey who's he? Can we sacrifice him? Oh my what if he's the wolf god in disguise! As a sheep! That's crazy! Oh my god he's going to eat us all! Slowly! Look at how he moves, it's... unnatural...

And what's around his neck?

Oh my god he's going to eat us all!

Slowly!

So I turned my back to them, watched the storm sway the trees, flatten the fields, watched the barn doors swing open, shut, realizing that I was free, sort of. I shook the ice from my fur, felt a chill, looked down at my muddy legs, remembered the purse, lowered my head and let the strap slide down, looked at the purse and wondered what was going through my mind? A purse? And then wondered if the sheep had been taking over, and then wondered if that could happen, my mind becoming all sheep all the time, envisioned an invasion starting from the brain stem, braincells like Mongol hordes, like Wild West Indians circling my cerebral wagon, shaggy braincells moving into my apartment, occupying my couch, uninvited.

Footsteps coming hard and I snatched the purse strap and trotted toward the fearful five. Hands grabbed the barn doors, struggled against the wind, swore and pushed the doors shut. It was dark. The hammering had changed its tone, was now heavy rain, and I figured the worst of it was over. Don't worry, I turned to tell my friends, but I saw that they'd been living in fear their entire lives. Oh well. I helped myself to some feed, which wasn't fresh. But oh well. Maybe it would be fresh tomorrow. I chewed, looked up, bleated, and they stared. Oh well. I ate some more. Eventually one came forward and pretended to eat, but watched me with her lovely dark eye. Oh well. And then a few others did the same. But the last one would not look at me, for she was a righteous beast, and she did not follow us as we huddled for warmth, lay down and lowered our tired heads, closed our heavy eyelids.

I called her Svetlana, the soft one that cuddled next to me, who had the lovely eyes. She was a bold ewe, only held back by a lack of life experience. Yes, we lay close. Get over it. And if, when early morning came, Svetlana and I quietly slipped into an empty stall and allowed our breaths to quicken, well, as I said once before, desire knows no bounds, and what happens behind barn doors stays behind barn doors.

The thrill of that, though.

## *Pigasus: Terror of the Night*

He descended from the rafters a fatted angel on black wings, grunted as his trotters torched soil and his wings furled along his flanks. "I should have known," I said, referring to the wings hidden beneath the cape. "Ingenious." When he spoke, his voice was surprising, deep, honey smooth, gentle even. But his breath smelled like bacon.

"We have unfinished business, Little Sheep."

"Really, call me Bones."

He laughed, said, "You will be nothing but by the time I'm done with you."

And I said, "You're overestimating my tastiness."

We circled each other while I thought out my

actions. I felt powerful, charged by past successes, my knowledge that I was Chosen, possibly immortal. With only a thought, horns sprouted from my head. "I should warn you, Pig, I used to be bison."

His wings suddenly unfurled.

"And I was the Black Death," he roared.

"Why, Pestis," I said, "I never would have guessed it."

The five sheep awoke, began to fret, and the cows inched forward. The cows needed blood for their milk, which was prized in twenty counties. "We lap it up like there's no tomorrow," they whispered.

We circled, and perhaps there were finger snaps from the chickens, whose fingers are a delicacy in many lands.

"Why did you do it?" I said. "Why did you murder those children?"

"Saviour of the young, are we?"

"I cannot bring back that which has been destroyed, Pig.

"Start with little birds first, Baba. It's easy."

We fought then, though who can say who rushed who, but soon I was on the Pig's back, gnawing at his neck. And then we were in the air, and he tried to knock me loose on the rafters, flew upside down but my teeth held on. The pig was enraged now, swooped low over the cows and I had to duck various stanchions and signposts and gate tops. But my grip never weakened and blood flowed from the back of the pig's neck. "I will eat your intestines before your eyes," he squealed in anger, now flying toward the roof. Through my teeth I said, "Do you mean that you'll eat my guts first, and then my eyes, or...?"

"You will see," said the pig.

We collided with the roof, went through the roof, kept climbing and soon were over the flickering fire-lit countryside, then through the clouds where the air was cold and the wind howled. The full moon cast embattled shadows on the pillow-soft cloud tops.

"I will defeat you, Little Sheep, and my evil legion of pigs and chickens and a few select goats will rule the world!"

"The only world you will rule," Pig, I hissed in retort, "will be a world of..."

"Of what?"

"Pain!"

We fell then, and our entwined shadow of wing and snout and fleece tore though the gentle clouds. We fell fast and it was all I could do to hang on as the smoke-filled air rushed past us and the flickering fires of the oppressed drew closer. Would the Pig kill both of us? No. He had a manoeuvre planned, for he was conniving. His wings would unfurl and I would have to hang on. Yes, and my teeth held firm.

But his flesh did not.

Well, that's the problem with those who are Truly Evil—they are in a state of constant rot. Their meat is held together by the loose bonds of decay and, though it is often forgotten, the only reliable way to defeat Evil is to spin it quickly, spin it till it flies apart, and do not let it huddle.

I'm sorry, Svetlana, but I have failed you and your kind.

I am not Chosen.

I am not immortal.

The last thing I saw before my snowy body sliced through the rafters of the barn was the black silhouette of the winged Pig. Saw it soar high and swoop down toward the sleeping city and heard its terrible cry as the pale moon shone between the clouds and the planet spun into oblivion.

*Morning has Broken, and No One can Fix It*

I nudged farewell to Svetlana, gathered my purse and left the barn. I bleated once to the sleepy others and they all bowed their heads, all except the righteous beast, who stood, turned her back to me, and kicked a little manure. Svetlana, however, did not understand farewell and followed me into the yard and I wasted a good thirty minutes trying to lose her. I tried little curtsies, head tosses. I tried hiding behind cattle, and farm equipment, but slowly she'd come round, keep close to my side. If I could have spoken, and if she could have understood, I would have told her, I'll be back soon, sweets, just have some business to take care of in the city. But, ewe that she was, she would have said, I know the score, sugar, I know you're playing the part of the rogue, the rascal, the *ram*bler. Just be safe.

In the end she didn't dare leap the wire fence. I should have known.

The storm had left the ground soft and my tracks would be easy to follow, but I had no sensations of being followed. I was invisible. Maybe this was a sheep delusion, a sheep trick to keep the heart calm. Or maybe it was instinctual, maybe no predator would hunt when the sun first rose after a harrowing attack by beast-shaped weather gods. Or maybe I just felt good? Couldn't be. I had a full belly, yes, and although my night had been haunted by dreams of Bat Moll my morning wake up had been warm enough. Sex is sex, and whether you're accountant or aardvark—if you're not getting any, you're not right.

But as my long shadow told me: you are a ruminating ruminant heading for ruin. And at best you are a petty thief, a scam artist, abandoned by everyone who never loved you.

Mornings, I've always hated them.

Glow fading, I headed to the river. I had often walked along the river with Weasel and knew there were train tracks when the shoreline was too steep to follow. So I would follow the rails to the city. And in the city I would... I had a phone, and I had a bit of money. If a sheep stole your credit cards, how quickly would you cancel the cards? You never know what's in a sheep these days. And the phone? But maybe they'd track the phone. Oh yes. Spy agencies would be on alert. Operation Ghanoush. Listen for the quavering query, attune yourself to the nasal accents. What is he after? God only knows.

I remembered the last time Weasel and I walked the river. Weasel had sworn off stealing shit, said, I want to be a stand-up guy, ha ha, no really, I want to tell some fucking jokes, man. But we knew it was tough to get into, what with the government security checks for comedians, the Prime Minister's

None Funny But Me law (well that's what everyone called it). And the vanished, I reminded him. But what if I changed my face and my name, Bones? You know, I could be Perry Ferret or something gay like that. You'd be good, man, I said, but you might have to go underground. Weasel kicked stones into the river. Aw man, you can't get rich underground. You just get dirty. Hey, speaking of which, how are things with your new girl? I squinted into the sun, sighed, said, I think she's tiring of me, Weasel. Tired of living with a gambler.

Gambler?

Yeah.

Oh, the lies we tell.

And the flat's too small.

It's a fucking room, man.

Yeah well she calls it *the flat*.

Know what? It's all good about getting some young pretty that's sweet and everything but...

Are you calling me old?

You're old bones, Bones. You creak.

We walked on.

Think we'll see a leg today?

Oh man, a fucking leg! Floating down the river!

A shaven man's-leg.

Sick!

Give us a joke, Perry Ferret.

Weasel stood on a washed-up pallet, declared himself Perry Ferret the Fairy Parrot and told the dead fishes to listen up, I got a joke for y'all. Do fishes have ears, man? Fuck, can't swim with like, ears! So, OK. These two trout go on a hunting trip, these two big floppy-eared trout in orange and shit and they're by a campfire smoking their pipes and they're like miserable because they can't shoot for beans, got bulby fish eyes and no hands and missed every bear they shot at, like aimed for a bear's furry face and shot a tree top. Didn't even hit a squirrel. So fuck, yeah. So one trout he says Karl, I'm so fucking hungry I could eat you, and Karl says Carl, I'm so intolerably hungry, and I could eat you, too. So then they like *hurl* themselves into the fire being all magmanamoose and shit and scream, Holy fuck my ears hurt Karl and...

Fuck, man, it's a lovely day, isn't it, Bones?

And you, you just can't focus, she said. I watched you from the flat yesterday, and it was so... typical. You're walking away head up looking at... who the hell knows. The sky? You almost walked into a parked car, Boney. It's just... sorry but it's weird. You're weird.

Should see me now, Babe.

Trains no longer used the tracks and weeds were beginning to shoot through the stone and tar and timber. The rails had rusted and wasps and grasshoppers buzzed or clicked across the gap. I kept a steady pace but found it difficult to walk a straight line. That was a sheep thing, I guessed, a need to look back while thinking ahead. Problem: sheep don't fear people and the closer I got to the city the safer I felt. It was big, and noisy, and it stunk, but I could get a good sheering and maybe some Chinese. And I could go to a movie. A good thriller, that'd be perfect. But of course you'd have to watch from a hotel room while eating your moo goo guy gross... throwing up everywhere. The sound of gunfire leaves you hiding in the washroom. Yes, there's pounding on the door, wolves in the air ducts.

*I think I'm going for cigarettes. But probably I won't be back.*

And I tried to clear my head of doubt, tried to move with confidence, tried not to think of my oblong shadow, those spindly legs, tried to remove the image of the black purse swinging below my vision. There are miles to go, so just be sheep. No, that's a trap, stay human, Bones. If you keep talking to yourself, man, you're gonna end up stuck in some craziness. I've seen it happen. Anyway, she leaves you, so what? Not saying I haven't been hurt, Bones, but what can you do but laugh? The government's got it right, but the fuckers aren't funny. Forgot this bullshit about dealing with problems because that's shit, man. I mean, if you laugh to the end you'll be someone who laughed till the end.

You're coming to an end no matter what, right?

Laughter, it's just... horror flipped over, like a cockroach.

I shook my head, feeling the voice of Weasel fade and the psychologist's flute warming up. But I didn't want that voice in my head, I was through with him, but something rustled in the grass along the tracks. It wasn't big enough to be dangerous, and wasn't fast, was just my shrink disguised as a porcupine, and he stopped, rose up a little, chittered his teeth and waddled ahead grumbling about years of study and ungrateful stupid scum and maybe I should have taken that job on Conquestador.

*I ask him if he knows the lifespan of a sheep.*

*Twenty years? he says. He's guessing. Likely it's the equivalent of a light sentence. Light for murder, of course. I'm thinking they'll keep you alive as long as possible. Or maybe not. I can't predict these things....*

The porcupine veered off the tracks, headed to the river. I followed, could smell the previous wanderers who'd taken this trail to drink or gaze at their reflections. At the shore I watched small fish, larvae, water striders. The porcupine, grumbling, continued along the shore. There were grasses, flowers. I nibbled. Maybe I should have let Svetlana follow me. I must be selfish at heart.

When I climbed to the tracks I was confused. Left or right? And that was odd because I knew the city was right, could see it, and if I were any good at climbing trees, I knew I'd see the distant hillside Constockade to the left, which was east, but still, I was confused. Who knows how long I stood in that spot before I realized my confusion was, in fact, alarm.

## *I Ram, I Ram so Far Away*

It was a thing of beauty, my response. It was what they feared, chewed their nails over, hollered and screamed about during later meetings when the technology was to be had, when the capability was there to make it happen. The scientists, all beauty school dropouts and failed magicians, who knew but one joke and could never get the punchline right, they said, Hey, it's a pig, or a cow, or a goat—

or a sheep, haha—what's the worse that could happen? And most everyone laughed. But the nail biters saw cattle convicts stampeding the fine crystal from their shelves, or swarms of goat gnawing their way through communications fibres and pigs, pigs en masse, fouling up pristine lakes and rivers. First our dishes, and then our phones, and then our water. Yet for the most part they saw nothing to fear in sheep, nothing other than a troublesome public desire to hug a thief, maybe, or to take one home. A man in the back of the room, whose sweater often itched, who had always remained silent, he did worry—about sheep sentinels—the heightened sense of smell, the discerning ears and worst of all, the lack of fear. They could move so easily amongst us. There's a sheep on your lawn, that's cute. And then one across the street: Look, they have one, too. Then three more. It will be the end of us. Good God stop the program now it will be the end of us!

He was locked away.

And the nail biters were dismissed, and the program went ahead, and men were put into sheep, sheep that slipped from their pens and could sense several dogs and men on the wind. Yes, four dogs coming from the east, with two Caucasian handlers coming along the tracks. And three more dogs coming through the fields from the south, and a fourth that was lost, on the trail of a rabbit. The rabbit, however, had evaded that dog, who continued its pursuit out of a misplaced sense of pride. The rest were picking up speed, leaving their pale handlers behind.

Energized, I estimated their distances based on the strength of their scents, hoofed lines in the dirt, did some simple algebra, saw that they would have me surrounded in seconds, so I kicked my woolly arse into gear, sprinted to the river and ran along the shallows following the muddy track of the porcupine while wondering if I/we could swim across and concluded yes but I/we'd be seen half way across unless I swam underwater but all this wool well we'd sink to the bottom where it would be quiet, so nice and so calm, just the beating of a heart, and that wouldn't last long either. But then you'd be just like that floating leg and then roasted mutton for boastful trout, so run Bones, run Bluebell-7, run up that slope where the porcupine is turning, hissing, saying, *What the fuck is up with you*, and leap the quills and get on the tracks again, and try to not to look back, because there will be nothing back there, you've lost them, they've stopped, are sniffing in circles, scratching their heads and asses, have wandered to the river and "I think it panicked" (you hear) "and drowned" (you hear) and "let's go home and get something to eat." Yes, don't look back, down the tracks, your future is in the city, Bones, and that's the city dead ahead.

\*

That was needed, of course. Breathtaking flight, edge-of-the-seat terror, and all the little lambs in the grandstand crying out, Mama, maamaaa. My horror of horrors story is nearing an end but there had to be another escape, another brush with death, another clever solution that's met with applause and then gasp, didn't see that coming. Forehead smacking, if anyone ever really does that. It's like waking from a nightmare and suddenly sitting up in bed. No one does that, either.

Happens to me all the time.

So it's late afternoon and yes, the city is in sight. It's what you imagine a city to be, all high rise and reflective glass, and it's seen from parkland, so there are dabbed-oil cottonwoods blotting out the lowlands, the slumburbs. And it's the future so let's have a few whirlygigs flitting over the city. Let's face it: if you can do the whole brain switcheroo surely people will have their own personal helicopters by now, tiny things just big enough for a fat politician's well-greased rear end. That's the future right there.

The park is lovely in the sunshine, and now night is falling. No one has seen you because you are soft of hoof and blend in so well with the topiary, fit perfectly behind kissing benches, ornamental glacial stones and commemorative statues. Earlier there was a lively border collie (is there any other kind?) chasing a frisbee and she stopped once, looked toward the hedges, tilted her head and made a move but was called back, Ellen, Ellen, frisbee, come on. Dogs. People think it's some sort of genetic wolf-fear that keeps the sheep in line, but the fear is fake. Sheep are lazy. Why worry about things when the dog will do it all for you? Act scared, they love it.

It's what worked when I met the stray, the one that'd chased the rabbit down the wrong hole (it was nothing but a culvert). The rabbit escaped and the master was gone and the pack, too—oh no doggy gone done it again, gosh darn, done went and dug down wrong gully, chased silly rabbit dog damn done it again—but he sniffed around until he caught a faint scent and next thing you know was face to face with it, the prize, the flesh-and-blood squeak toy named Him. Told to go get Him, and got Him.

Him acted very frightened of the mean dog, the fearsome Johnny Good Boy Killer. Him backed away on trembling legs. J.G.B. Killer growled just to see the chill in Him's eyes, the weepy heartslop. But what were the orders again? The problem was, they told you one thing one day, another thing the next, go for the throat, go for the leg, go for the arm, too many damn limbs. Him was cowering now, making an awful sound like crying and doggy don't like dumb whimper, so stop it, stop it now, but it was clear enough to see the effect it was having, the eyes searching left and right, so I continued the low, pathetic bleat, which sounded like a mortally wounded bagpipe, and when the hound finally looked away I pulled a trick out of the ugly goat hat and rammed hard into that doggy skull and left the hound dazzled and reeling.

Did I run? I did not.

When night fell in full bloom I pulled my purse from the bushes and left the park and its streetlamp shadows for the gloom of the strip malls and industrial parks, listening closely to every crunch of foot and clink of glass. I had no point of reference, no response other than a phantom shoulder shrug to the question, *How dangerous is it for a sheep to walk the alleyways at night?* Wait, does the sheep have a purse? At first I kept to the tracks, paid little heed to the passing trains, caught the odd double take from the windows, but no one would shout halt, for everyone had a destination, and before long the trains stopped running. The city. So many people in people bodies. Don't think about it, Bones.

I knew this part of the city well, moved quickly, slipped between stopped trains and walls, kept to the hidden side of workers, leaped to the subway platforms and up stairwells and maintained a quick pace. A sheep moving slowly is suspicious, but a sheep moving fast is a delusion. A group of homeless drug addicts were playing hopscotch in the dark and I trotted past them. A woman in a wheelchair was holding a fallen man with a bloodied lip and I trotted past them. A cop was lecturing two young boys on loitering near a parking garage and I trotted past them, nothing more than a part of their shared dream.


### *Cats and Rats and Elephants*

Trees, hedges, fences, parked cars, dumpsters—soon the sheep knows what the mugger and the guerrilla know: the inner city is a skulker's paradise. And in this haphazard land a sheep with black purse might as well be a chameleon, or a shapeshifter. And dogs, once encountered, for they are encountered, they are city dogs and know nothing of chattel. You're a big ugly cow-dog or something? Got any smokes? And cats, well let's not mention cats, the Prime Minister's hatred of cats led to their being driven from the land years ago, rounded up and herded onto barges and set adrift for the land across the sea.

But that's another story.

Being home, seeing everything from so close to street level, seeing it through a wide-angle lens, made me feel like a child again. I'd have to stretch to get a letter in that mailbox, reach up to unlatch this gate, jump a little to see in shop windows, and I missed Georgie at my side, though Georgie was never a city dog. The city was still very much asleep, traffic was light, the odd laughing drunk couple exiting a taxi. In an alley I passed a sleeping homeless man, came back, picked a pack of chewing gum from my purse and left it with him. The alley led to a leaf-riddled square—it was early autumn here—and the square would lead to a row of townhouses and the very last townhouse, the brownhouse, a lush house which seemed to be held up by the other, more sober houses. I lived here.

Past tense.

Cop stops me: name, address?

Bones Mansheep. One Hilltop Pastures Way.

Eyes me, squints, says move along now little sheep.

In the square a woman sat on a bench, tapping her foot restlessly. She wore heels, a short skirt, had bruised legs but muscular calves. She checked her phone, clicked her tongue to upbraid her late rendezvous. I knew her, but had never known her name. I moved quietly behind her, caught the streetlight glint of her jewellery, sought to slip silently past, but maybe it was the leaves, or maybe I smell strange (though no stranger than her fading soapscent), but she turned, started to say *who* but finished with a not-so-holy *Jesus*, which was followed by a curious head movement, as if someone had poked her between the eyes.

"You're off the drugs, so why are you seeing a sheep with a purse?"

She reached out to see if I was real.

I made the sheep sound and she smiled, said, "Oh my dear god, I have to take a picture of this."

The phone flashed and I kept on moving, turned the corner and strolled down the sidewalk, crossed the street and didn't hide, for this was my neighbourhood and if anyone passed me, zombied drug addict or restless insomniac, I'd nod my head knowingly, keep my head high, strut along aware that anything is plausible in this brave new world of ours, that people have accepted the new forms, that one day we'll take an animal sabbatical, just to get in touch with our true nature. Oh, what are you? An eagle? You know, I always thought I was a deer, but my beastiologist he says I'm a gazelle, and you know, they're not deers at all. And then it goes beyond that, as a manager you've been much too timid, and our previous did leave his brown bear behind... so... we're not pressuring but... sales *are* down... And of course actors and actresses will be fawning over the roles of Old Yeller, Bambi, Black Beauty...

The brownhouse, two vacancy signs, one of which hung in the cracked window of my former room at the rear. Why had no one moved in? Could I get in? And then what? Sleep. Sleep and wake and splash water on my face, run my fingers through my hair, vow to *never* take that shit again, swear at Weasel, or Goose, or whoever they were and lose my balance and catch myself on the bookshelf and the books spill out including all 20 volumes of *The Insane Adventures of the Mates of Mayhem* and I slide down the wall, babbling, begging for the straightjacket to be a little tighter please. No, no, don't let the world call you back, Bones, don't go there, don't sleep, have you lost your sense of purpose? And then laughter and the flagstones that lead to the backyard path, the swinging gate, the muffled sound of music.

Oh yes, Froggies is still open.

So a sheep walks into bar...

Really, it's that easy. There's no doorman, no ferryman, no one to pay off to let you slip behind the fibreglass toad from which hangs the daily special (*sorry kitchen closed*), from which you watch the scattered shadow patrons, the half-blind bartender, the flickering TVs—and you know you hear it, smell it even, the sounds and stink of former friends. Yes that could only be Weasel's cackle, and in quiet moment... a honk? And you half expect to hear Mother's incantations but she's long gone, rest her addled soul. You stay to walls, slip behind the bandstand, move from table of stacked chairs to table of stacked chairs, watchful for shards of glass and the smell of spilled beer making you ill. Here you are, Bones the Sheep, framed for sins you never committed, soon to be face to face with your moment of redemption, and what will you do? Burn the place down? Jump on their laps, lick their faces? Does anyone realize how easy it is for sheep to infiltrate a popular pub?

I watched them from the booth across while lying in the shadow under a table.

Weasel pounding their table, laughing at anything Hog dribbled out, something about trunks and elephant sex, and Goose was pointing a finger at the blond dude, the new Bones. The blond Bones listened, shook his head, drank his beer. I began to feel off-kilter, lack of sleep perhaps, or food, or an excess of strangeness, people, the night, my old haunts, and I thought when was the last time I cried? I don't know why I thought that but then I thought when was the last time I laughed or told a joke? And then I wondered why the hell I wanted to laugh or tell a joke anyway? In a perfect world no one laughs, no one needs to make anyone laugh, it's all just fucked up make believe therapy, right Weasel? Was Weasel looking at me? What if I showed myself? The ridicule. What if I followed them, one by one, into the loo? First the fake me, whoever the hell he was, blond Bones, the Play Prison Playmate. What's my killing technique? Hooves or headbutt? Kick his feet out as he pisses and kick his head into the urinal as he falls. Goose next, comes to check on fake me and bends over sees the blood and out of the stall

I sprint, spin and deliver two hooves to his throat. Who's after Goose? Weasel? Hog?

Fuck it.

Weasel had looked away, had stopped laughing and was gazing into his empty bottle. He'd lost weight, if that was possible. He needed new clothes and I'd never noticed the grey in his stubble. Hog was waving his hand in Weasel's face, holding money and gesturing for Weasel to get another round. Weasel considered his empty bottle then stood and when he returned I was at his side and it's fucking Bones, guys, he said, it's fucking Bones and they didn't believe it, and then they did, and cheers went up. They wrapped their arms around my shoulders and rubbed their knuckles into my head and the blond Bones slipped away, was never seen again. We met each and every night at Froggies and no one spoke of the sheep, for this was safe haven, this was where we planned our revenge on the government, our raids on their banks and factories and, one day, the CCC itself. We lost Goose in there and Hog's left hand was severed, but our fame grew and Goose's funeral was an underground sensation. And riots spread across the land as man and animal rose up against the arseholes in power. Cattle blocked the highways and pigeons chose immolation over migration, found pigeon heaven in fighter jet turbines. The government tried to flee but we caught the Prime Minster and his top lackeys hiding in the sewers and we thanked our sponsors from Wicklow for the shiniest of blades, the tricky bastards hardly felt a thing.

A sheep on the national flag.

No, a unicorn.

Yeah, that's fancier.

Sheep's an embarrassment.

Well really it was just a mascot, we did all the planning.

More often it was a hindrance.

And stunk!

Weasel fell into a coughing fit, a cough deep in his lungs that didn't stop. Goose, saying, "Don't fucking infect me," pushed Weasel to the floor and stepped over him, gesturing for the blond Bones to follow, which he did.

Lastly, Hog helped Weasel up and, shoulder to shoulder, they carried each other into the predawn pallor.

## Robyn's Hood

It was remarked upon in several sleepy morning coffee shops and select office gaggles, chuckled out by the lucky few who had been chosen to see it, the sheep in the subway, the sheep sauntering down Sixth Street, head low. Someone said, Did it have a purse? 'cause I was on the S-train one of the workers he said, after I said good mornin', he said to me Hey as long as I don't see a sheep with a purse tonight. And another worker said, Maybe it's the one that held the bus hostage?

Oh my god! I forgot. Do you think?

But by noon the story of the errant sheep was forgotten—just another animal in the news, just another joke on the lam—though one woman swore to her apologetic john, and she had photos to prove it, that she was visited by a little lamb as she sat waiting, waiting, and just about the time she told herself she was dreaming the lamb returned and would you believe dropped a purse in my lap, she told him this as he counted out bills, said, The thing pulled out a sandwich bag with a business card in it, then pulled out a phone and next thing I know I'm calling this number at six in the goddamn morning saying, Uh, hello, I have, like—do have a name, honey?—well it didn't want to give me its name. Then the woman on the other end, she says is it a goat, a cow, a big dog—and I'm thinking I'm losing my mind, tell her, No, darling, it's a lamb, and she says what colour, what size, and I say how many critters are going to have your business card, sister, and she says can you bring it here, and I was just about to hang up, some prank, right? So I tell her, No, I'm working, so she gets me to write down a number and call a taxi—but only this one special taxi, absolutely do not call another taxi, all stern and all, and who the hell is she, right? But whatever—I do it. Story of my life. Sleepy guy shows up, gives me a twenty to not talk about it, sheep says bah bah before getting in the van and why are your pants still on, honey? Hurry please. I need sleep.

\*

In the back of the taxi, and he knew the driver, a boyish, broad-shouldered man with fine hair and a sniggering bald spot. The driver yawned, looked back two or three times, "Trying to recognize your eyes," he said. "Can't quite place them. Did you escape on your own, or did an operative help?" The sheep neither shook nor nodded its head, as the question's form negated response. The driver worried about plants, as he called them, but he didn't think that'd happen until the procedure was reversible. Though maybe it was already. Maybe it'd always been. "Well, lucky you weren't caught, eh?"

The sheep smelled like beer.

And the last time the sheep had seen this taxi man? He was hauling away the very one he was now leading him to. How long ago was that? The sheep lay down in the back of the van and slept in fits and spells as the van wound through the city and the driver kept chatting, saying PETABBY would come back strong, but for now they had to keep their heads down. He grumbled about finances, having to work. "And that woman, don't know why I do this. Does she even know how much gas costs? Please don't shit in my van." He seemed to need to talk, and maybe he only talked to Constock. Maybe he'd write a book about it ten years from now when the foolishness faded, when he could crow a little about his sacrifices. At his side, those he rescued. Maybe this very sheep. Petting it. Now muttering something about fucking politicians and convicts while the sheep half-dreamt of luminous forbs, muttering something about his vegan revelation while the sheep twitched and sighed, muttering more about lousy convicts and building a commune and razorwire fences, clean food and clothing optional and "Free love, hey, whatever happened to that?" But the sheep was out, was leaping in the glowing grass when the van door rolled open like a peal of thunder.

\*

It had started to rain. Wren dressed me as a Siberian husky—fake muzzle and a kind of dog toupee, a tail attachment and a yellow doggy raincoat over it all—and leashed me, led me to the fourth floor of an apartment building, knocked on door 42 and said, "Chow, puppy, my meter's running." And then the locks were undone and the door opened slowly and it wasn't tall Robyn who stood on the other side but another Shetland sheep who looked an awful lot like me, and then I heard her voice, Robyn's, saying, "Move, will you? They'll see." And the sheep moved aside and Robyn reached for my lead, pulled me in.

She sighed. "Who do we have here?"

I was quite taken by the other sheep: she was clean, bright eyed, wore a fuchsia kerchief around her neck. She made herself comfortable on the brown leather couch and watched as Robyn removed my disguise, complained about Wren's sloppiness, for my tail was upside down, commented that someone needed a bath and then said, "OK, are you hungry?" I stared at her. She'd put on a little weight, but seemed healthy. She was wearing black yoga pants and a burgundy sweater. Her black hair had a streak of red, was straighter, longer. "Hey, pay attention," she said, taking my face in her hands. "You may have been a big bad guy before, but you're a little sheep now. Are you hungry?"

"Bah," I said.

"Of course you're hungry," she said.

"Are you hungry, too?" she asked the ewe on the couch, who didn't respond. "No, you're just going to watch him, aren't you?" Robyn whispered: "I think she's got her eye on you. Careful."

She filled a bowl with oats, sat on the floor, rested her chin on her palm and said, "You may have to stay here a while, all of the halfway farms are full." I wondered why she wore lip-gloss, foundation, mascara. "Are you cool with that?" I nodded. I mean, did she still see me as a man in sheep's clothing? She motioned to the couch, said, "Heather isn't 'Stock, you know. She's all sheep. We got her during a botched...." She took my face once more. "Unbelievable," she said.

"Heather, come meet the reason you're here. This is who we *meant* to grab." But Heather didn't move, and I just kept eating, and so Robyn sighed, said "Bones, Bones," told me her story, of being a child on a farm, having pet chickens, she was so young, and then a fire, the barn falling, the city, of growing so tall so fast and the money she made as a fashion model, then the thing she didn't want to talk about, and then depression, an overdose of sleeping pills and meeting Wren in the hospital. "He was a disillusioned intern, they were courting the best doctors, doing awful things though, like brain exchange. And there I found it, Bones, my purpose. We met weekly, integrated others, we trained hard but Wren was so sexist, 'women can't run, women can't throw,' oh he made me so mad. Yeah, sure, I had a lot to learn, modelling didn't prepare me for this, but I knew animals so well, and I got in shape again, and I just kept on Wren day after day. It was so exciting, Bones. They were really doing it, putting murderers in these poor creatures, and then it wasn't even murderers. Yesterday Wren sent a text. Tax evasion. We really thought we'd bring it down. It's evil, it won't last. No, it's not evil, it's a joke. But it wasn't a joke."

There was a PASCAL poster over the couch.

People Against Suffering and Cruelty to Animals and Livestock.

She got up, started making tea. "Is there anyone you want me to contact, Bones?" I shook my head. "That's sad," she said. I shrugged, sort of. "You'll sleep in the den with Heather, if that's OK? Some 'Stock don't take well to non 'Stock but you don't have a choice here. She's sweet, though. Quiet, tidy. But no hanky panky. Does it look like I have room for lambs here? I'll put pants on you. I'm serious. Once we get a farm, maybe, but this apartment is the last place they'll look, so for now, at least until spring, this is where we stay."

"Bah."

She sat with her tea. "It's a good cause, I tell myself. But I have to take care of me first. It was like, I was part of a cult, you know? There was nothing more important than PETABBY, but we fucked up over and over and you realize, these guys, they're all just lost sheep too, and in the end they only care about being part of something, and it wouldn't matter if we were saving the world or outlawing the colour red. You know?"

"Bah."

"And activists," she sighed once more, "they're boring. They just spew what everyone's been telling them. They're no different from the lawyers and bankers and cops they make fun of. I mean, they'd make jokes, too, saying let's stop the fuckers and put them in pigs and ponies and they just didn't get it. I'd yell at them, You just don't get it, and they'd be like, Whoa, dude, chill.

"If we got in power we'd be no different than what's already there. Do you know why?"

"Bah?"

"Right! Because we're all the same.

"So, I am out of it, done. I want to be far from here, want to never hear the news again, the mindless *junk* and thrilling *bullshit* and breakthrough this and that and the sick desire for violence and retribution and I want to be that little girl again, Bones, in a field, dressed like Little Bo Peep, looking for tails to tack back on my lambkins. I want a farm, and a flock, and some sun. And maybe Wren will join me. Am I asking for much?"

"Bah. Bah."

What else could I say?

## *I, Ewe*

It's spring now and we've driven out to the countryside, an old boarded-up farmhouse and an orchard left to grow wild. Robyn drives through young green grass, parks the van behind the house, slides open the door and Heather and I leap, frolic in the sun, finally out of the apartment, finally hooves in earth and not treadmill rubber. Robyn follows, keeps an eye out for police and predators.

Winter was long and often mindlessly dull. I spent the days reading anything I could get hold of—literature, history, science, psychology—learned to turn pages with a little Stickum on hoof, would discuss it all with Robyn using a child's Spell and Speak. And when I felt sheepy I snuggled with Heather, gazed at the pasture posters on the den's wall, created names for all the little lambs.

And slept.

But one day Robyn came home with a modified keyboard, big keys, no thumbs required. At first I wrote angry letters to the gang, to the media, would have to fight past sheepy acceptance, but rage, when I found rage, did not help things. So the letters became satires, anonymous jokes and spoofs sometimes posted to subversive websites and always quickly pulled down, but not after dispersing like birds. After a while I signed my work BS, for Bones Sheep. Soon I had a following, an audience.

The acceptance, after all, is part of me. I've grown fond of, even protective of my sheep half.

You could say we've become attached.

And where would this body go?

"If I can swing the mortgage," Robyn says, her arm sweeping across the property, "this is where we will live. Would you like it here?" She's talking to Heather while I follow behind, nibbling on the green-green. We climb a small hill. At the top of the hill there's a tree and in a perfect story it's ripe with apples, but it's not ripe with apples, it's in full bloom. Bees buzz all around us. Robyn reaches for a blossom, breaks it off, places it in her hair, then does the same for Heather, behind the ear, but it doesn't stay.

When it falls, they both bend to pick it up.

Fuck that's beautiful.

## *An incomplete list of acknowledgements*

Many thanks to everyone who encouraged my little sheep along the way and/or gave feedback, especially:

Michelle Butler Hallett
Kerry-Lee Powell
Nancy King Schofield
Carol Steel
Dave Skyrie
Elizabeth Blanchard
Kayla Geitzler
Edward Lemond
Elaine Amyot
Danny Jacobs
Nick Voro
Beth Janzen
and Jeff Bursey

I brought a draft to the Banff Writing Studio in 2014, where Tamas Dobozy and Dionne Brand were invaluable.
And yes, thanks to the Canada Council for the Arts and the New Brunswick Arts Board.

And Rick Harsch, for giving this a chance.
And Cindy, my love, for giving me one too.

L.T.

Lightning Source UK Ltd.
Milton Keynes UK
UKHW010632280223
417789UK00001B/141